Praise for
John S. McFarland

"Authentically unnerving. An uneasy pleasure to read" —Ramsey Campbell, author of *The Influence* and *The Doll Who Ate His Mother*

"In *Baby Monster* McFarland revisits the cursed town of Ste. Odile, where the darkest angels of our souls, *all* our souls, reside." —Dacre Stoker, author of *Dracul*, and great-grand-nephew of Bram Stoker

"A really unusual and impressive collection—harrowing but frequently quite touching. I very much admire the elegance, the old-fashioned elegance of the writing. McFarland has a talent for finding something touching on the other side of horror. My admiration for McFarland's work is sincere." —T.E.D. Klein, author of *The Ceremonies* and *Dark Gods*

"I genuinely wanted to re-read this one for pure pleasure. Some powerful and disturbing imagery lurks within." —John Linwood Grant, author of *Where All is Night, and Starless*

"The writing is spectacular, by the way. I was drawn in from the first sentence (which is always the goal, right?) and find the language very sophisticated & descriptive." —E. J. Hammon, author of *Ted Bundy: Memories of the Beast*

"The stories absolutely absorbed me. These stories will swallow you whole." —David B. Busboom, author of *Every Crawling, Putrid Thing*

"McFarland's stories are like gifts, sprung from a dark chest full of wonders. Historical horror...horror against a wide variety of cultural backgrounds... Whatever story you pick up, it may remind you (in pieces) of Ray Bradbury or other great masters of the genre, but it contains one thing for sure: McFarland's unique vision and his very own voice! A true master among writers working today!" —Michael Schmitt, Wandler Verlag

"This is a beautiful and terrifying collection...A beautiful darkness penetrates every story. I will read this book a couple of times to absorb it all. Really amazing." —Shelby Scott, *Scare You To Sleep* podcast

"McFarland tempers his frights with the mercy of familial love and sympathy for outsiders and victims. Horror readers will be riveted." —*Publishers Weekly*

"McFarland is adept at creating unsettling scenarios within very human, everyday contexts. The horrors that plague his characters feel like something that could happen to anyone at any time, which is a great way to creep under a reader's skin and stay there a while." —Philip Fracassi, author of *Behold the Void* and *Boys in the Valley*

"McFarland's style definitely whispers of older writers, like Lovecraft, but his handling of language is much more crisp and focused. The perfect combination of the literary and contemporary. One of the great, undiscovered talents of horror fiction." —C.P. Dunphy, Gehenna and Hinnom

BURNED MAN AT NIGHT

Pensive Horrors by
John S. McFarland

JOURNALSTONE
YOUR LINK TO ARTIST TALENT

ISBN: 978-1-68510-164-0 (trade paper)
ISBN: 978-1-68510-165-7 (ebook)
The Library of Congress Catalog Number has been applied for.

First printing edition: October 24, 2025
Published by JournalStone Publishing in the United States of America.
Cover Artwork: RF Pangborn
Interior Illustrations: John S. McFarland
Edited by Sean Leonard
Proofreading and Cover/Interior Layout by Scarlett R. Algee

JournalStone Publishing
1400 North Wood Rd.
Murphysboro, IL 62966

JournalStone books may be ordered through booksellers or by contacting:
JournalStone | www.journalstone.com

To my wife Cindy, who has put up with all of this.

CONTENTS

INTRODUCTION

WHAT'S IN A SURNAME? Quite a lot, it seems, especially if you're a writer of horror fiction. Just ask Arthur Machen, Robert Aickman, and Shirley Jackson. The mere mention of some surnames evokes praise and approval in equal measure, as well as conjuring up all manner of feelings and opinions: *hallucinatory, dreamlike, mental disintegration, unsettling ambiguity,* among other descriptive plenitudes.

John S. McFarland is one of those names, and not to mention one of the best-kept secrets in horror fiction today.

I first encountered John's work after posting on social media about my ongoing love affair with *Rod Serling's The Twilight Zone Magazine.* The magazine, like the TV show, had a profound impact on my early years, and not only as a young, aspiring writer but also as a person. Many of the writers who had appeared in its pages had become near-mythical beings to me. So, here I was, talking to John S. McFarland, who at the time of his published story *One Happy Family* in the October '83 issue, had been a newly emerging talent.

I struck up a friendship with John, albeit an online one, and shortly afterwards I introduced myself to his first two collections, *The Dark Walk Forward* and *Baby Monster.* And I soon came to realize that John was a one-off, a lone wolf prowling a territory very much his own.

John has an uncanny knack for writing turn-of-the-twentieth-century tales that perfectly capture the times. Although distinctly written in his voice, it was interesting to note his fiction contains various elements reminiscent of Flannery O'Connor and William Faulkner.

In all honesty, I believe John may be one of the few modern horror authors writing today whose work is set entirely within another century. Think of the literary version of the film director Robert Eggers, and you're partway there.

In this, John's latest collection, *Burned Man At Night*, we once more return to the fictional St. Odile, a small backwater town in the state of Missouri.

What a place!

Ste. Odile palpitates with dusty anguish, a town in the perpetual birth throes of bloodstained transformation, one whose geography is as wrought by its phantasmal influences as its inhabitants.

Here you'll find a panoply of crumbling family dynasties, cursed lovers, and hopeless criminals. Interestingly, many of these characters intersect with one another, emerging and fading, respectively, into the background of preceding storylines. It's this kind of narrative ingenuity and world-building that is worthy of King or Straub.

In this proto-Lynchian town of misfits, working people cling to ambitions as obsolete as their wretched dreams, while the financially ailing upper classes pursue philosophical doctrines often to their own undoing.

In Ste. Odile, there is a veritable pantheon of characters: miners, baseball teams, and surgeons, all battling away against maledict inheritances, generational abuse, and supernatural monsters. It is an elegant mix that unfurls like a magnificent tapestry.

Even when we, the readers, are lured into stories not set in Ste. Odile, the Missouri town's shadow extends far beyond its borders, which is a testament to John's ability to fully immerse us in his world.

John's love of pre-twentieth-century history is very much evident on every page of every story. Fashion, entertainment, medicine, and technology collide in exquisitely realized detail.

More than this, his characters sing; that is to say, they're elegiac and haunting and monstrous, terrifying in their operatic elegance and coarseness, hypnotizing despite their decaying psychologies.

John's prose is at once realistically drawn, and yet, because of the times he writes about, there's an almost otherworldly quality in his eloquent illuminations.

In his latest collection, **Burned Man at Night,** John navigates us through such chilling stories as *A Burden of Dust, Seeping Towards Gehenna, The Intercession of the White Worm,* and the eponymous *Burned Man At Night.*

The authenticity at the heart of each story has made me question whether John has, in fact, kept secret his power for channeling the voices of lost souls to his aid when writing.

Most of all, I would like to say, McFarland is a surname that belongs alongside Laird Barron, Ramsey Campbell, and Gemma Files, gifting us a special kind of horror fiction we rarely see these days.

—Frank Duffy (Warsaw, 2025)

BURNED MAN AT NIGHT

SEEPING TOWARD GEHENNA

I BELIEVE IT WAS old Socrates who said physical beauty is but a short-lived tyranny. What else would an ugly little wart of a man such as he say? If it is a tyranny, it is one all wish to be subjugated under. I have accepted this 'tyranny' as I move without effort through my life, attuned to the resentment of filthy peasants and poxed cacodemons around me.

I dance as if in a masque among them. The pestilence that is killing them off has not touched me. In Riquewihr, Strasbourg, Bennwihr, and elsewhere where the Death was rampant, I was undefiled by it. Yes, Nature has divided me from these filthy throngs, that I may give them the suffering their vile lives warrant, beyond that spread by this contagion. Perdition slowly absorbs them downward, toward itself, during all their misbegotten lives. It is preordained. They have no recourse. I speed some of them on their journey.

For the moment I trade in toads. I took the old man's cart from him last night. He choked on his own blood after I cut his tongue out. He had made a living selling the toads to simpletons as a cure for plague. His cart is complete with the rotting corpse of a victim of the pestilence on a shelf he had built, and a box holding the toads that eat the worms emerging from the putrid flesh. Since the toads suffer no ill effect, the old man, whose name I have already forgotten, convinced the peasants that eating the toads provides protection from the disease. I took his tongue as an extra talisman to peddle. He gurgled impotently for a few moments, and died. I meant to let him live because somehow, I rather liked him. I have already forgotten his name. I have had many professions. This one will do for now.

Ah. This is the road to Colmar. A larger town. I thought of climbing the hill to Zellenberg, but surely someone would recognize the old man's cart there. He was a resident. I will do a good business in the larger town, I think. And if there is an open burial pit there, I will replenish my supply of toads.

"The sheriff lets you cart around a plague victim?" The voice startles me. I turned to see a ragged boy of ten or eleven addressing me.

"I have not seen the sheriff, nor any of his men. If I do I will tell them I am doing charitable work, which I am."

"What charitable work?"

"What business is it of yours, boy? Who are you?"

"Gilles Chauvet. My family is dead. From the pestilence."

"My cure here could have saved them."

"Perhaps I should have it?"

"It isn't free. I would guess you have no money."

"If your work is charitable, it should cost nothing. Are you another miracle worker taking people's money? Who are you?"

"I am called Merton of Riquewihr. That is as much as you need to know. You seem to have a brain in your head, I must say."

"I have lived in that town since early winter. I have never seen you there. You are more fair than most. I would have noticed you."

"You are a keen observer. I must go now, lad. I have business in the west." As I walk away the boy calls to me.

"You must not have heard. Ulrich of Wurttemberg, the master of all these lands, is coming to Riquewihr. He thinks of it as his new home. If he knew of your cure..."

I stop. "Wurttemberg is coming here?" I turn and look at the boy. I feel I am becoming suspicious of his cleverness. Still, he could be useful. It is rare to have the opportunity to meet such a high and influential personage as Wurttemberg. "Hmmm. What a patron he would be. Tell me, boy, how are you at catching toads?"

"I will show you," the boy says.

I turn the cart around and we head back down the hill to the Valley of Alsace. At the crossroads we go south to the open burial pit. Ravens circle above the fetid crater. The heat of the day has permitted the stench to seep through the lime scattered on the wrapped corpses. Two of the ravens land in the pit and begin tearing at the exposed skin of some of the corpses.

"Isn't it an odd thing that the birds would eat these dead people?" Gilles asks. He is very dispassionate. It is merely an observation, not a judgement.

"No," I respond. "It is necessary. Every creature must be expected and allowed to act according to its own nature. I believe that is in the Bible."

"Can you read?"

"Yes. I have something of an education."

"I have taught myself a little. It isn't a thing I need, but I am curious."

"Much to learn in this world."

"Is cheating people your nature?" Again the boy makes no judgment.

"That and many other things. Everyone seeks survival and comfort. Only trust them so far as you do not impede those things. Neither trust them beyond the point where your destruction will benefit them. Is cheating in *your* nature?"

"I think it must be."

I suspect that the parts inside of him where qualms and regret would live are missing. I also suspect this about myself. And so, I have acquired an accomplice.

The death pit is nearly full enough to cover with dirt. The mayor and sheriff will decide this. "Move along the edge of the pit and collect a few toads from the bodies. Just get what you can reach from the edge." As I say this, the boy walks out onto the rotting bodies as indifferently as if he were walking a garden path. "I see you have your own method..." He collects a few of the toads hopping atop the corpses or sitting still on the putrid faces waiting for worms to emerge. Having collected five toads, he makes his way back to the cart.

"These should last for a while," he says. He drops the creatures into the wooden box under the corpse we carry. "Perhaps we should get a fresh one," Gilles says, examining the body. "This one is old and spent... and there may be no worms left in it."

"Very well. We will pick a new one."

I pull the carcass off the shelf upon which it was displayed and drag it to the pit. As I do this, the boy struggles to pull a fresh body by its feet up toward the cart. I help him and together we pull the corpse up to the cart and place it on the display shelf. I remove two toads from the box and place them on the dead face. "She was a young one," I say, as I situate the toads.

"It's my mother," the boy says.

I make no response to this. His indifference seems at first odd, in one so young. Odd, at least, unless he despised her. But I suspect that he finds grief unuseful. The lesson on survival and comfort I tried to teach him seems to be an already familiar notion to him. Emotions which do not abet our existence and prospects are pointless. Most men never learn this lesson. This young boy knows it already. To understand this is a true epiphany. "Come," I say. "Let's head north."

The vineyards on either side of the road are sadly unworked. No peasants attend the grapes or the grain fields and all are dying. A little boy of three or four approaches us. He is pale and thin and seems exhausted. He stoops every few steps and pulls bunches of wild leeks and yam stems out of the ground and stuffs them into a satchel. "That is Roland," Gilles says. "He is an orphan too."

"Gilles," the little boy says, "are you coming to supper today?"

Gilles looks at me as if I were to answer the question. "I don't know," Gilles says. "I think so." He then addresses me: "He is collecting greens for supper. The Sisters of Perpetua make two meals a day for orphans if we help gather the things they need."

"I can't pull anymore," Roland says. "I'm tired." His head droops as he says it. He looks as though he may collapse.

"You have enough there," Gilles says. "You need to get it back to the sisters." He takes the little boy's satchel and throws it onto the toad box. Then, with some effort, stumbling backward at first, he lifts the child onto the rear of the cart next to the box. Though he sits next to a corrupted corpse, the boy seems undisturbed.

"His family lived near us beyond the North Gate," Gilles says as I pull the cart. "He is afraid of the dark so most nights he sleeps with me in our old house. We hide from the sheriff's men because we don't want to go to the orphan home."

"But that is where you have your meals."

"Sister Euphemia feeds us in the kitchen. The home is too crowded. She doesn't care if we live there or not."

He has answered my question and I have heard as much of his story as I need to. Or want to. A pack of wild dogs chases a mare and her colt across a dry field to the east. Animals are starving these days. I look back to the north and see an unwelcome sight. Two armed men on horseback. The sheriff's men, approaching us. I have been lucky in avoiding them up until now. "What are you doing with that body?" one of the men calls. Both are older than thirty, I would say. One has red hair, the other black.

"Performing miracles," I respond. "You see the toads perched on this dead face? They catch worms and slugs from the body, which transforms them into cures or talismans for the pestilence."

"Personal possession and transport of a plague victim is against the law," the redhead says.

"Drop the body where you stand and the collector will pick it up. Or answer to the sheriff and risk arrest," the dark-haired man adds.

"My only wish is to save lives," I say, bowing to them. But I do as they demand. I pull Gilles' dead mother from the shelf and lay her at the side of the road. The two men ride on and I continue our journey.

"Perhaps," Gilles says, "we can sell the toads without the body to catch people's attention?"

"That will have to be our plan," I agree.

In another hour, we have arrived at the south gate of the town of Riquewihr. Just off the square to the east is the hospital where the Sisters of Perpetua care for dying victims of the pestilence. Next to it is the home for orphaned children, also administered by the sisters. I stop the cart at the open front door.

Roland is asleep in the back of the cart. He looks as frail as a newly-hatched bird. I wake him. He sits with much difficulty. I lift him from the cart. He cannot weigh more than a couple of *livre esterlin*: less than a spadeful of horse manure. That is the space he occupies in this world. I give him his satchel and he shambles unsteadily to the door of the orphan home.

"Wurttemberg is staying there," Gilles says, pointing across the square to a street of prosperous houses. "With d'Estang the new mayor, until he finishes his plans to buy property and build his house."

"Which house is the mayor's?"

"The sixth one on this side."

Uncertain whether I will need the cart again, I decide to keep it a while longer. The street ahead is called Austregisilus. I have not seen it much in my earlier wandering around the town. The houses are large and grand and well kept. Servants shake out sheets and empty chamber pots in the street. The sixth house is well-timbered and four stories high. I drop the cart at the front door and knock. An old woman barely taller than Gilles opens the door. "What is it?" she barks.

"I have been urgently told his Excellency the Duke of Wurttemberg is visiting the mayor."

"Yes. What of it?"

"I wish to save his life and guarantee his health. I carry a cure in this box of common toads which, when cooked, are a shield against the pestilence."

"Agg!" the old woman throws up her hands in disgust. "I'll send one of his servants." She closes the door.

"Do we wait?" Gilles asks.

"We wait."

"It might be," the boy continued, "that I should hide. I look too much a beggar. Perhaps Wurttemberg nor anyone in his company should see me?"

"Stand against the wall here." I direct him to an alcove to the right of the front door. He steps into it. "You are right, boy. We do not know if this is a charitable household or not."

"I doubt I would be charitable if I had the means," Gilles says.

"It just prolongs misery."

"And serves no purpose if it has no benefit to me."

"Very true, boy, and wise of you, too. Mankind is diseased and broken. All of us...are sliding toward damnation throughout a lifetime, if we know it or not."

"Yes?"

"Since we cannot help but be fallen, whatever gives me comfort and advantage in this moment is what matters. There is nothing else."

The door opens again. A haughty, slim figure which I can identify as neither man nor woman stands there, towering over me. "What is your business with the Duke?" a nondescript voice intones.

"To spare him from the pestilence." I reach into the box in the cart and remove a fat toad. "Consuming these creatures, which I have especially treated and raised, will provide immunity."

"This town!" the figure says. "Full of such nonsense. My master is not a fool. In these sad times he wants distraction and amusement, not a grandmother's superstitious remedy. I need one who can bring him laughter. Find a jester, a fool, a dwarf or a town idiot. Then I might let him receive you." The door slams.

I look at Gilles. "I suppose we should ply this trade in another town. When word gets out that Wurttemberg refused us, so will everyone." I turn the cart around and start to pull it toward the square.

"But perhaps," Gilles says suddenly, "perhaps we should go back to the orphan home."

"Why?"

"To look in on Roland, if he is still there. It's at the south gate. Will only delay us a moment."

"If it just takes a moment. We must get back to the burial pit before it is covered over. It surprised me a little that you care to look in on him. It doesn't seem to be in your nature."

"I understand why you would see me so. I have heard rumors that in Spain and the north of France, the nobles have found a practical use for the orphans."

"Yes?" We walk toward the sunlight of the square. A few peasants can be seen passing one way and another near the fountain.

"It is said there are those whose craft is to create from an orphan or foundling whatever the noble desires."

"I have heard of this."

"If the lord wants a dwarf, the child's bones are broken and reset to make a dwarf. If he wants a fool, the child's face is cut to an eternal smile or frown. Backs can be broken to make a twisted cripple. All for the amusement of the lord."

"You want Roland for such a use?"

"He serves no other purpose. It will improve his lot. And we will make money."

"We have nothing to dull the pain."

The boy shrugs. If I believed in such things I might think he and I were meant to find each other. We quickly reach the door of the orphan home. I knock. A well-fed nun opens the door. "Good Sister, we wish to take Roland with us to gather greens, if he is about."

"He is. I kept him in today because he is not well. I am hoping his meal has put him right. I am not sure he is strong enough to go out."

"I promise to take the best care of him. He knows where the most succulent leeks are and we need him to show us."

"Very well, then. We are needing more greens." Sister leaves us at the door and returns a few moments later, guiding Roland by the hand. The boy looks a bit steadier on his feet, but still weak.

"Where are we going?" Roland asks.

I lift him into the cart. "To see what Nature may provide," I say.

We leave by the south gate. It is now late in the afternoon. I look back at Roland. He is asleep again. Gilles plods along next to me, barefoot in the dust. "Where will we do this?" he asks.

"I need tools of some sort. There is an abandoned farmhouse at the fork of the Zellenburg Road. We might find something useful there. It will be dark by the time we get to it. No travelers about. It is isolated enough that there should be no one to hear his cries."

The sun is setting over the western foothills as we arrive at the overgrown farmhouse. There is no one to be seen on the road. I drag the cart to the front door, which hangs half-open. I hope there are candles or an oil lamp so I may see to work on Roland.

I push through the collapsed door and step into the farmhouse, leaving Gilles outside. To my relief there is a table toward the rear of the single room and three stubs of candles positioned on it. I see a cleaver and several large kitchen knives on a smaller table against the rear wall. "Let's get him in here," I say to Gilles, stepping outside. He stands at the rear of the cart.

"He's dead," Gilles says dully, dropping the frail hand of the carcass.

"Damnation! Of all the sarding bad fortune!" I swear.

Gilles pulls the dead boy off the cart and pushes the body with his foot into the weeds. "Lots of leeks here. He found them again," Gilles says.

At this moment, of course, the obvious remedy to my situation occurs to me. The obvious one. I consider it for a few seconds. In no more time than that, I am certain it is the simplest solution. From behind I grab my young accomplice by both his scrawny arms. "What are you doing?" he asks dispassionately as I lift him and carry him into the house.

"What I must," I say. "Our subject is of no use anymore. You are here. You are now the subject. To apologize for the pain you must endure, I will not do. I must break bones and cut your face. I must. To pretend to regret any of it would be an insult to your natural cleverness. I am not certain, but I suspect you deserve better than that." I place him on the table.

"I think so," he says emotionlessly. "I won't run away. You are right. You *must* know that *I* understand."

I look at him a long while. It might be affection I feel. I cannot tell. I smile. "You do understand, my small friend. This I know. You understand more than most, that we are the bane of nature, the butcher of animals, the playthings of demons, forsaking our birthright to our more diseased patrimony, all the while crawling...seeping toward Gehenna."

A BURDEN OF DUST

"FORTUNA'S WHEEL MAKES VICTIMS of us all." Cleander Redburn Weatherill, age twelve, mumbled this to himself. He was sitting on a weedy, sere hillside along the dirt road called the Hopewell, under an enormous catalpa tree. His Aunt Calliope's washed-out gravel drive emptied onto the Hopewell Road, and it was there, under the great tree, where Cleander always sat and waited for expected company to arrive.

Cleander was a little ashamed of himself for adopting what he thought of as a backwoods custom, of waiting by the road or on the porch for company. How bored, how ignorant, how devoid of creative or intellectual pursuits does one have to be to do that? He asked his aunt this question when he first noticed the Nixons across the road doing it. She had no answer. She had never noticed it. Now, a few months later, he understood it better.

Cleander's father was to blame for everything. His mother and himself were perfectly happy in Newton, Massachusetts, near Boston. His mother Hestia had her church activities and paranormal investigation group. Cleander had libraries, archives, museums, and most of all, his mentor Edmund. Edmund had been his tutor when Cleander was ill for all those months. As a mentor, Edmund introduced the boy to weird literature in the form of E. F. Benson, LeFanu, Machen and many others. He broadened his concepts of history, science, mathematics and most importantly, imagination. Having been born in Tibet to missionary parents, Edmund introduced Cleander to the mysteries of *Vajrayana* as a means of mastering his fragile physical being and taking command of his inner self and the cocoon of awareness that surrounded him through life. Cleander proved to be an incomparable student.

Edmund encouraged Cleander's inquisitiveness and writing aspirations. He resolved to help the boy to publish a journal of weird fiction to be called *The Stylus* in honor of Poe's never realized magazine. Edmund promised to collaborate with Cleander on a tale to be called *The Death-Messenger of Neferneferuaten*, just before

Cleander's father was mustered out of the Army and announced his plans to his family.

Floyd Weatherill finished his service at Fort Dix after the world war. He was anxious to begin his civilian life. Floyd predicted there would be a land rush down in Florida, and he believed by cleverly buying and selling real estate, he could make his fortune. By 1922, he decided the time was right to act on his plan. The only available property Floyd could afford was in a town called Oscola, which, to his disappointment, was more than a hundred miles from the ocean. After a grueling, days-long drive down nearly the entirety of the Atlantic coast, the family found that the town of Oscola could scarcely claim to exist anymore. There were a few wooden buildings along the state road, but the main remnants of the old town lay down a county road, rotting and abandoned on the edge of a fetid lake in swampland. Cleander's parents died there. If they had not, the boy was certain it would have been him instead. Cleander had imagined that he could pick Edmund as his guardian and return to Newton but the state instead gave custody to Calliope, Hestia's sister and the boy's closest living relative.

And so, Cleander found himself living with a maiden aunt in an empty region of fecund desolation, a land of cornfields, haystacks, dirt roads: an essentially unpopulated vista of scrub hardwood forests and fallow fields, of wide distances and indefinite spaces fading at every horizon. Lost in a landscape so undiscovered and unremarked that any slight change or aberration drew immediate attention. Having never been so alone as he was now, he sat under the catalpa tree and watched the short treetops to the east, looking for dust rising above the circumscribed limits of the oaks, indicating that someone was coming. Cleander thought that the sight of a dust cloud rising from the woods was a portent that at that moment there was a possibility of some stimuli, however small, impacting another featureless day.

Cleander thought he would put himself in a meditative state to pass the time. He did this often, every day when possible, so that the power he had attained over his physical self would not weaken. But, today he decided not to meditate. He wanted to watch the road. Two vultures circled above the treetops to the east, in the vicinity of the crossroads, the general store and the salt spring. There was often roadkill, a racCoon or opossum splayed in the crossroad.

Cleander's red journal, with the words *A Journal of Aeons* written in black ink on its cover, sat on his lap. In it he had hidden the last letter he'd received from Edmund ten days before. Cleander unfolded the letter.

My dearest Cleander:

I know you feel lost and alone, but you are not. In my mind I am with you every day and the psychical bond we have made together cannot be broken or diminished by ignorant interlopers. Yes, I received official notice from your aunt, as your legal guardian, that I must stay away and have no physical contact with you. I must comply, at least for the moment. An officer acting on behalf of the sheriff of Oscola County visited and questioned me regarding the circumstances of your parents' deaths. It was as nothing they had ever seen: a few scraps of flesh, bone and clothing. Although they expressed suspicion about my 'influence' over you, in their wildest imagination, they could not construct a scenario in which you could have borne any responsibility; the devastation of the bodies was so savage and complete. The fact that several other disappearances have happened since, in the vicinity of Lake Oscola, dissipated their suspicions toward you.

Since I cannot visit you for now, I have arranged to send you a gift which will keep me in your thoughts until we can be together again. The beauty of monstrosity in Nature was often a topic of our discussions. Particularly the monstrosities of the sea. Since moving to the California coast, I have found possibly the most hideous creature in creation. Anarrhichthys ocellatus. The so-called wolf eel. I have recently befriended a naturalist specializing in Pacific sea life and he introduced me to the species. He has a preserved adult which is the most monstrous creature I have ever seen outside a nightmare. It is over eight feet long. Its black eyes are unfathomable, yet malevolent; its horribly gaping mouth, lined with savage teeth, seemed to me to serve for a stinking portal to Abaddon (my host laughed at this), and their mottled, wrinkled skin is the color of plague corpses. In other words, they are just your line of country! I purchased from this gentleman two living juvenile specimens which, at some considerable expense (!) I am having shipped to you.

You will need a tank of salt water (35 parts sodium chloride per one thousand parts water) as large as you can find. The creatures can grow to an enormous size in the ocean, but in captivity will only grow to a size that accommodates their environment. They prefer echinoderms and shellfish as a diet but, I am told, will eat almost anything. They are young and therefore a bright orange in color. Their hue deadens as they grow. The delivery service I hired told me that the crate should be at your door on August 10.

Despite your aunt's objections, I am sure we will be together again someday. I may have a surprise bit of information for you soon. Up until a certain moment, I will resume my fortunate duty of acting as mentor, but soon after, our voyage of discovery into lands of wonder and mystery will be led by you.

Always,

Edmund

This was the day the eels were due to arrive. Aunt Calliope warned Cleander that she had no use for pets, especially fish, especially ugly eels. She said she would let him prove to her he could care for such creatures and keep them out of her sight, but that this was only a trial and if there were any problems she would demand he dispose of the fish. She made many threats that she did not act upon, but she had become more irritable of late. She provided Cleander a ten gallon stoneware crock to keep in his room, and prepared the salt water according to Edmund's recipe.

Cleander placed his journal on the ground beside him. He wondered what the surprise Edmund spoke of might be. Immediately a plump yellow and black caterpillar plopped onto the red cover. He looked up into the branches. From where he sat, he could see at least a dozen catalpa caterpillars feeding on the leaves. "This is what I will feed the eels," he said. He brushed the caterpillar away.

He thought he heard the pop of tires moving over gravel and a transmission grinding to the east. A cloud of dust arose over the diminutive treetops. Cleander stood. In another moment a green panel truck with the words Liberty Delivery Service on the side emerged from the tree line. Cleander rushed back up the drive to the house. The truck followed him, stopping at the end of the drive near a concrete walkway that led to the kitchen door at the back of the house. The driver was a thin man in a khaki uniform. He stepped out of the truck. "You the kid a-waitin' fer this?" he said.

"Yes," Cleander answered.

"Hope I don't have to do this again," the driver said. "Haulin' live animals is bad enough, but fish! Shit on a shingle!"

"I don't care for swearing on my property!" Aunt Calliope had just stepped out the kitchen door. "Especially in front of a child! What kind of hillbilly example is that?" Cleander didn't know her age. She was older than his mother, nearing fifty, but looked older.

"I do 'pologize, Missus," the driver said.

"Miss."

"Sure. I fergot myself there fer a minute. Worried about keepin' these ugly sons-o'... about keepin' these things alive."

"Can you help us get 'em inside?" Aunt Calliope asked. The driver nodded and negotiated a rubber-lined and lidded crate out of the back of the truck onto a four-wheeled cart.

In Cleander's small room at the front of the house, the crate was carefully settled to the floor. Cleander removed the lid. The smell was rank and overpowering. The creatures inside were about ten inches long. One was a bright orange color and the other more pallid and listing to one side. "That one is sick," Cleander said.

"I'm surprised they both ain't dead," said the driver. "All they been through! I got a pouch of food they been a-eatin' too." He removed a flat tin from his back pocket and handed it to Cleander.

Aunt Calliope signed a form the driver removed from the crate lid, tipped him a dime and showed him to the kitchen door. In the kitchen, Cleander heard her rummaging through her cabinets. She returned to Cleander's room holding an old colander. "Catch them with this," she said. "I ain't gonna touch 'em."

The boy took the colander and scooped the ailing fish out of the crate and into the crock. The healthy one was more difficult, but after a few minutes was captured and lowered into the crock also. As Aunt Calliope emptied the stinking water from the travel crate a saucepan at a time, Cleander opened the tin of food. He dropped a few morsels of mysterious maroon flesh inside it into the crock. The healthy eel snatched it immediately. The pallid eel appeared to be dead. After watching the creature for a few minutes to be sure it was lifeless, Cleander took the dead eel up by its tail and threw it out his bedroom window.

The living eel seemed energetic and active. Cleander dropped more food into the crock and the eel ate it ravenously. "I will call you...Ugallu after the demon servant of Tiamat the sea monster," he said. "Edmund did this for a reason. There is purpose behind this gift. I will have to find something else to feed you, Ugallu. There are swarms of caterpillars on the catalpa tree. I hope you like them..."

In the following weeks Cleander forgot completely about his routine of meditation. The power he had once mastered over his frail body seemed of secondary importance to the care and observation of his ravenous and increasingly hideous new pet. Ugallu ferociously devoured the caterpillars the boy fed him and it was soon obvious that the creature was destined to outgrow the crock holding it. "This creature is more than a pet. There is a purpose, some mystical reason, no doubt, that Edmund has sent him here." Cleander whispered. "That is something he would do! He mentioned a surprise to come. It must have something to do with this animal."

Edmund's next letter arrived on August 25:

My dear Compatriot:

I suppose I should be glad that at least one of the eels survived. Sending them was something of a precarious proposition, I knew, so I am happy with a 50% success! My biologist friend tells me that feeding your Ugallu the catalpa caterpillars is a stroke of luck. They are possibly the best thing it can consume. The tree itself is known in folk medicine for being a source of unrivalled medicinal use. Your creature will thrive on those worms and its growth will, as a result, accelerate. I do not know how to advise you on its future care! I am sorry about that.

I am sorry also that your aunt continues to cause you distress. Minds like ours must expect in this life to be at odds with those with no vision or imagination. I am sorry to hear you are not writing or meditating these days, but the distractions of daily life can detour us from our purpose. The level of mastery you achieved in the Vajrayana was as nothing I have seen before. Though your abilities may wane with disuse, you will always retain some awareness and contact with that other, shall we say, dimension, that other plane of being beyond this one. You broke through, my young friend, and you can never go completely back again...

The heat and drought of the season were relentless. As the end of the summer approached, Aunt Calliope had grown tired of the crock in her nephew's small room. "This thing is too big for this crock. It has to go. Enough is enough!"

"We have to find someplace else to put him," Cleander protested. "I don't want him to die."

"You had that thing long enough. I put up with a lot with you here: them books you read, that pagan trance you go into. I put up with all of that. I'm at my limit. *At my limit*! This is my house and I make the rules. From now on you're gonna help more and behave like a Christian boy...and get rid of that ugly damned fish!" She stormed out of Cleander's room and returned out the kitchen door to the backyard where she had been snapping green beans earlier in the morning.

Cleander knelt next to the crock. He knew this time would come, but had formulated no practical plan for any action to take. He looked down into the dark water at his Ugallu. The creature was now longer than the diameter of the crock. It had changed from a bright orange to a somber, almost nondescript gray. Edmund had predicted this, but it seemed almost miraculous and unique to Cleander. He doubted that any other fish of this species could transform itself so completely. The creature pushed its fanged mouth out of the water, as if it sought attention from the caregiving boy. Cleander touched the narrow ridge between its black eyes. He did this often when the fish rose to the surface of the water.

As he knelt, watching Ugallu, Cleander felt a numbness in the right side of his skull. His temple throbbed a little, his small room seemed oddly like an illusion, then he felt as if an avenue had just presented itself to his awareness. He was in a region of simple perceptions, of rudimentary need and basic stimuli. There were no subtleties, no questions to ask or answer. There was nothing but *being*, the undoubted fact of existence. Surely these were the primordial, essential processes within this creature's awareness.

Edmund's prediction had come true. The gate Cleander opened through his mastery had not completely closed. There was a connection now between a rational mind and a rudimentary one. It could never consist of more than the stimuli of need, hunger, satiation, temperature, sight, sound and perhaps a trace of some calming familiarity. But it was most certainly, to Cleander, a connection. At that moment, it seemed, the creature had permitted the union.

The boy sat motionless on the floor for a while, trying to decide what to do. He thought he sensed fear, or survival response in the creature, but now he was less sure that he wasn't imagining it. "I won't kill you," Cleander whispered. "I won't throw you into the bushes to die. You need more than I can give you here. You need space to grow. You need salt water..." An answer suddenly presented itself. "The salt spring! The large pool there! That's where you will go."

Cleander presented this idea to Aunt Calliope. She seemed less than interested. "If you can get it down there alive, that's fine. It's a quarter of a mile. I don't see how you'll do it. I just want it out of this house. I don't give a good goddam what happens to it."

The next morning Aunt Calliope had a Ladies Sodality meeting at St. James' Church in Potosi. She was usually gone for hours. Cleander saw his chance. He walked across the dusty road and knocked on the Nixons' door. Dooley Nixon, long retired, answered the door. He was a stout, short man of about seventy. "I'll swan if it ain't Mr. Weatherill! Ain't seen you in a coon's age, buddy!" he exclaimed. He seemed genuinely happy to see his young neighbor.

"Morning, Mr. Nixon. Sorry to bother you but I need a favor."

"Oh? What kinder favor?"

"I got this saltwater eel in my room in a crock. Aunt wants me to get rid of him. I want help to take him down to the salt spring and let him go. In one of your trucks, if we could."

"Well now, I see your aunt ain't home. Is it alright with her?"

"Sure. She doesn't care, so long as he's gone."

"How big is the crock?"

"Ten gallons."

"How big is this critter?"

Cleander held his hands apart at an indeterminate and varying distance. "Sixteen and one quarter inches."

Nixon nodded. "Ok. We'll put it on my old flat wheelbarrow and onto the flatbed truck. Be easier. You run on and bail out water until it's yay deep." He marked a place on his wrist. "I'll be over yonder, here direc'ly."

In twenty minutes' time Nixon and Cleander had carted the crock through the house and onto the flatbed he had backed into the driveway. "Never see an eel like that before," Nixon said, truly aghast at the creature. "Ugly peckerwood, aint he?"

Cleander smiled and nodded. He climbed into the cab of the truck.

Nixon drove as slowly and carefully as he could. The road was partially washed out in several places and he was trying to jostle the crock as little as possible. "I ain't got much to do of a morning," the old man said. "Mabel visits her sister over in Lesterton a lot. This give me somethin' to do."

"Thank you for helping me," Cleander said.

"You know, son, it ain't nothin' much livin' in that salt pool but bugs and such. What is this eel of yourn gonna eat?"

Cleander frowned. "I didn't know that. I thought he could catch fish and frogs, and those catalpa worms...I guess I'll have to make sure he has food."

The salt spring flowed from the ground near the southwest corner of the crossroads. It emptied into a pool nearly a hundred feet long and fifty feet wide. At its eastern end the water seeped into a creek known as the Saline, and made its way for many miles to a salt marsh at the edge of the Mississippi River below Ste. Odile. Nixon parked at the water's edge. Cleander helped him as best he could to slide the crock from the flatbed to the ground. Together they tipped the crock, and its contents poured into the salt pool.

Ugallu flopped out of the crock and into the pool. Cleander watched the creature slide into the water and as he did, he sensed a feeling of freedom and familiarity. Ugallu hesitated near the bank for a moment, then disappeared into the pool's depths. Nixon put the empty crock back onto the flatbed. "Well, that's the best you can do for him," he said. "He ain't used to winter, I guess, but fish survive it in lakes and ponds."

"Thank you, Mr. Nixon," Cleander said. "I'm going to walk home. I want to stay a while."

"Suit yerself, Buddy. I'll drop the crock off on yer porch." Nixon nodded at the boy and climbed into his truck.

Cleander sat on a rock at the edge of the pool. He could sense Ugallu moving around, unseen in the deep water. The creature seemed to the boy to be bewildered by the great space it now occupied. "I will visit you every day," Cleander whispered. The sound of a screen door slamming caused him to look back toward the general store across the dusty crossroad. Mrs. Cook, the proprietor was sweeping the porch. Cleander looked back to the pool. "I will bring you food every day," he continued. "Whatever I can find. I will serve you. I know I must serve you...until I know *why* you are here."

The supply of catalpa caterpillars would last a few more weeks. After that Ugallu will have grown too large and would need something more substantial. Cleander watched the water for another hour. Aunt Calliope sped through the crossroads in her Studebaker and didn't notice him sitting there. "I had better head home," he said to the still surface of the water. "But I will come every morning to feed you, and I will sit here with you to write and meditate. You won't be alone."

When Cleander got home, Aunt Calliope was furious. "I told you to collect them boxes of jars out of the garage and wash 'em."

"I was going to do it. I took Ugallu down to the salt spring."

"'Gonna' don't get it done. I got canning to do and you're *gonna* do chores here or *you'll* be livin' in the salt spring."

Cleander found the three splitting cardboard boxes of jars in a cobwebbed corner of the garage. Stacked behind the boxes were three old wooden box traps his grandfather must have made, for catching rabbits, raccoons, and opossums. Cleander carried the jar boxes out to the wash house spigot near the back edge of the yard. He rinsed them out carefully and placed them in the sun nearby.

In another two weeks, all the caterpillars were gone. On a Thursday morning Cleander carried the last bucket of them down to the salt spring and pitched them into the pool. The black arch of a mouth lined with sharp teeth exploded again and again through the surface of the water and enveloped the wriggling food. The boy sat on the large rock which had become his rostrum from which to communicate with Ugallu. "You have grown so much!" Cleander said. "I can't see all of you at once but you must be four or five feet long at least, and growing faster than is normal for your species. You *are* special. I *knew* you were special." A muscular crescent churned the water, preceded by a glinting rayed fin. The serpentine form flashed in the sunlight for a second. "You are strong. You are prospering. I hope to have something more substantial for you tomorrow from the box traps. Something warm-blooded like nothing you have had before." As Cleander sat on the rock, imagining the movements of his creature in the deep water, he sensed need rising up from below. There was a remaining dissatisfaction. There was still hunger.

Cleander had stowed his *Journal of Aeons* inside his shirt. He removed it and a pencil he had brought and began to write.

The great creature continues to grow. I hope to start feeding him small mammals by tomorrow or soon after. I sense that I am communing with his consciousness, but I know not with certainty what eldritch awareness or understanding he may have. But I do believe I have broken through.

"Cleander!" It was Aunt Calliope standing in the roadway just above the crossroads. "I have told you and told you! I never laid a hand on you yet but I swear if I have to come down here again to fetch you to your chores I will wear you out!"

Cleander jumped to his feet. "I'm sorry, Aunt Calliope. I just like to spend time with Ugallu. And I have to feed him."

"How would you like to grow up in the orphanage? Huh? I could turn you in tomorrow if I wanted to!"

The next few weeks were cooler than early August had been, but in September the heat returned with a vengeance. Cleander made his trips to the salt spring shorter to avoid antagonizing Aunt Calliope. But often he got lost in meditation or speaking, in his own mind, to Ugallu, and forgot the time. He decided that in a few years he would leave Hopewell and the farm and Aunt Calliope and join Edmund wherever he happened to be in the world. That would be his last resort. He hoped circumstances would change and allow him to join his mentor sooner.

The first time Cleander caught a rabbit in a box trap, he carried the still trapped animal down to the spring. He placed the trap on its end on the ground, opened it, and the rabbit leapt out and escaped. The next morning he found he had caught an opossum. He thought of clubbing the animal to death before fully opening the trap door, smashing it like churning butter, but knew this would be too savage and cruel for him to do.

By the time Cleander dragged the trap down to the salt spring he had decided to try a communication with Ugallu to make the creature aware that prey was coming and that he would have to catch it. At the water's edge, Cleander emptied his mind and repeated under his breath: *"Come near, and be ready. Be ready."* The boy held the string tied to the top of the trap's door in his left hand along with the trap's cross piece on top, and held the back of it in his right. With nearly more energy than he possessed, he swung the trap back and forth several times for momentum, then finally, at the apex of the motion, he pulled up the sliding door. The opossum ejected from the trap wriggling in midair. Before the animal hit the water, a great dark head and hideous mouth emerged and snatched it. The opossum squealed slightly, a sound mixed with the snap of breaking bones. The huge snakelike fish churned the water a moment, its coils breaking the surface and crashing down again.

Cleander was astounded at how large Ugallu had grown. "Edmund was right about the worms," he said. "Edmund was right."

The trapping of animals went well for the next few weeks. Through mid-October, Cleander caught prey almost every night. The next morning after his chores, he would drag the trap down to the salt spring and feed his beast. He would then sit on his rock and talk to Ugallu, in hopes of receiving some communication back from the depths. One morning when the weather had turned cooler again, the boy thought he sensed frustration. "I know you are still hungry, my friend." He whispered. "One small animal is not enough. You are growing and growing and you must brace yourself for cold weather, for hibernation... or whatever your race must do in winter. Know that I am feeding you as best I can. I must set more traps. There is nothing more important to me now than your survival. I will serve you, I promise!"

Cleander carried the trap back to the fallow field just beyond Aunt Calliope's backyard fence. He baited it with persimmons he picked up from the ground under the tree near the wash house. He checked his other traps and found them empty.

As he entered the kitchen door Aunt Calliope was waiting for him. She grabbed his arm and shook him. She had hardly touched him at all in the months he had been living with her. Her face was red with frustration and he had never seen such anger in her eyes. "I told you to haul those rotten planks out to the dump!" she screamed. "I nearly stepped on a copperhead this morning living in there." She raised her hand to slap him but didn't. "One more chance, you little damned orphan. One more chance and I swear I'll just leave you in the middle of nowhere."

Cleander composed himself as she released his arm. "Ugallu is a gift from Edmund. He is a special being. I sense it from him. I would rather live with Edmund, but I must care for Ugallu. He depends on me. He urges me."

"I swear to God I think you're goin' crazy! You seem crazier and crazier. I ain't gonna take care of a damned lunatic!" The telephone on the kitchen wall rang. "Get outside!" Aunt Calliope commanded. Cleander heard her tone change dramatically as he exited the door and she answered the telephone. "Gracie, good morning. I was gonna let you know I have extry jars you can borry..."

That night Cleander sat on his bed, focusing his thoughts on Ugallu:

I will not abandon you. Not even for Edmund would I do such a thing. You are a being come here for a purpose. You are my connection to primal things. In those things lie knowledge and understanding of aeons old, essential things most of mankind can never know. It is blocked from them by their so-called 'civilization'. I know now that we do, indeed, communicate. You have accepted the offering of my consciousness. It is an honor. You must survive. To do so you must become the great beast it is in your blood, your inheritance, to be. Every small creature I give to you was born into the world for one purpose only...to sustain you.

Edmund sent you to me for the purpose of our mutual survival. He knew you must grow in the wisdom of the ages from which you have emerged and that my sustaining you would save my life. Edmund knew this. I know he would sacrifice all to give me this understanding.

Cleander awoke earlier than usual the next morning. He pulled on his overalls in the dark and stuffed his journal into them. He moved quietly through the house past his snoring aunt sprawled across her bed in her bedroom.

The grass, crabgrass, and clover that covered the back yard were very damp. Cleander's brogans were thoroughly wet by the time he reached the pasture gate. The autumn constellations, Andromeda, Perseus, and Cetus spun coldly overhead. The boy thought it ironic that Cetus should be looking down on him this morning as he had spent the night in concentration on his charge, the writhing servant of Tiamat in the salt pool.

Cleander found all his box traps empty except one. The door was sprung, but as he lifted the trap he was disappointed to find how light it was. The skittering noise inside it was virulent. The boy lifted the lid slightly and saw a single rat inside. "This will have to do for now," he said. He started the walk down the dark road to the salt spring.

The captive rat thrashed about furiously inside the trap. Cleander had never walked the road in the dark before. He stumbled in washed out gulleys that had formed over the years across the forgotten road, nearly dropping the box trap each time. He knew Ugallu was waiting for him.

Be patient, Ugallu. Great Ugallu of the cold depths. I am sorry I have so little for you this morning, but if the traps are sprung later today, I will come again...

The crossroads was dark except for a tiny measure of silvery starlight. One faint light could be seen through a window of the general store: the one illuminating a display of Oh Henry candy bars on the countertop. The salt pool was black and nearly silent but for the faint trickle of the salt spring.

Cleander walked to the rock which had become his ordinary seat.

Ugallu, be prepared.

The dark water churned fifteen feet from where Cleander stood. The boy pitched the rat into the water. The wriggling animal was snatched a second after it hit the surface. Cleander sensed dissatisfaction.

I'm sorry, Great Ugallu. I will bring more later if I catch prey. I promise you.

The waters fell silent again. The black trees surrounding the crossroad were becoming gray. Cleander sat on the rock and watched the water and listened to the few early morning sounds to be heard. Birds were chirping. The whippoorwills were going silent to acknowledge the coming day. As he could see better, he began to read through his journal. This was a record of the person he once was, before he came to Hopewell. He had noted in it a telephone number at which Edmund could be reached at Bodega Bay. Some day he would call the number. He needed to hear his friend's voice again. He felt that every day he spent apart from Edmund was missed opportunity and wasted time. Cleander noted how his creativity had suffered, as well as his imagination and how his mastery of the *Vajrayana* had weakened to the point he could not be certain he could do anything beyond communing with his Ugallu. And even that connection seemed sporadic and questionable.

As the morning sunlight began filtering through the trees warming his back as he sat, Cleander heard the screen door of the general store slam. Looking behind him, he saw Mrs. Cook sweeping the porch as she began her day. As he turned back, he noticed a black striped lizard trying to warm itself into ambulation in a spot of sunlight. Cleander grabbed the reptile, which was still incapable of escape. "I'm sorry," he said and tossed the lizard into the water. The creature was snatched from below with a slight disturbance of the pool's surface.

Cleander tried to focus his thoughts on the mind of the fearsome totem enshrined in the saline pool.

Now you are more than you were when you first came to me. It was necessary for my survival here. I made you more than a creature of the sea. Fearful humans must create their own sanctuary from fear and helplessness in the universe. Man made god, and I made you. Great Ugallu. Yes, I sustain you as humans sustain god only by belief. But more than that, you sustain me. You need merely food. I need myth, spirit, hope, understanding. You provide these because I ordain that you do. But also, you give the consciousness of ages, of the elemental that I may better understand my own existence.

"Cleander!" The crunch of rapid footsteps on the gravel of the road diverted the boy's train of thought. It was Aunt Calliope. She rounded the corner of the crossroad with rage in her expression. "This is the last straw, boy! If you was my own kid, I'd yank you bald-headed!"

Cleander ignored her and said nothing. His gaze remained on the surface of the water.

You are now Leviathan, Cetus, Great Ugallu. You are a messenger of lost ages, aeons! You have grown, strengthened. Even I cannot conceive of how great you are now.

"But you ain't my kid, so I'm done with you. You had eggs to collect and chickens to feed, and here you are. Man of leisure, not a responsibility in the world!" She approached her nephew and grabbed his arm. "I'm talkin' to you!" She stood in front of him to block his view of the pool. "I got half a mind to wear you out, sheriff or no sheriff!"

You must be strong, Great Ugallu! Do you hear me? You must demand and take what you need!

A green sedan skidded to a stop in the crossroad. Cleander thought his concentration must have masked the sound of its approach. The rear door of the car swung open and the boy heard a man's voice say: "Let me out here! This is who I am looking for." A handsome young man in a tan suit carrying a single valise emerged from the cab. It was Edmund! Cleander could not believe his eyes. His imagination was strong. He doubted what he was seeing. This was the surprise of which Edmund spoke? "Cleander! It's really you!" Edmund said. "At long last!"

"What in God's earth?" Aunt Calliope said.

"Edmund...Edmund!" Cleander was nearly dumbstruck.

"So *this* is your Edmund?" Aunt Calliope scowled. "What are you a-doin' here? You was told to stay away."

Edmund advanced to Cleander and hugged him tightly. "I'm here, my friend, finally," Edmund said. "You are Aunt Calliope? I am here because I have a lawyer friend back in California who says there is a way to transfer guardianship of this boy over to me. I felt certain you would be interested in this possibility. Especially if I presented it to you in person."

Aunt Calliope grabbed Cleander's arm. Edmund tried to remove her grasp and the three of them stumbled closer to the water. "He's my kith and kin," Calliope said. "My sister's boy."

"You don't want me here," Cleander said.

"I been to some expense with this kid," Calliope went on. "I need something for my troubles. From you or your state, the govermint...somebody!"

A great wave undulated across the water's surface. Only Cleander could see it. A dark, sinuous specter arose from the wave. Cleander was astounded by the coiling cacodemon poised like a cyclopean shepherd's hook. The monolith glinted in the morning sun and was the color of a long-dead corpse in a hedgerow. Cleander had never been afraid of his creature before. The boy's expression of awe and fear caused his aunt and Edmund to turn and see the looming beast. As Edmund shrieked in terror, the great mouth closed over his head and shoulders. The chasm of the mouth was enormous, gated by rows of jagged teeth lined before a gaping maw of pink, gray and a darkness blacker than Abaddon.

ICE STRETCHING TO DARKNESS

ANSE WAS TOLD BY his professor of engineering at the Moravian school at New Herrnhut that he would regret the day he gave up his studies and returned to Tukkat his home village. Regret was indeed the right word to describe how Anse had come to feel in the last few months. He realized now he had just been homesick at school, that the sudden urge he had then to honor the traditions of his father and grandfather and return home had been the biggest mistake of his twenty-eight years. The Moravian school was gone now, he heard, and with it his chance for a new life and career in Copenhagen, or wherever luck and hard work would lead him.

Instead he returned to a village hundreds of miles to the north to fish and hunt seals, to trap foxes and start a family. Tukkat was a real village then. Corundum deposits had been found on the Nares Strait a century ago and the village grew up above the rocky shoreline, around that industry. Canadians, Norwegians, Swedes, Americans and Danes came to work the mines. The local Inuit were found to be unsuitable for the repetitive manual labor underground. There was a population of nearly two hundred people at one point, but when the corundum reserves were found to be limited, the inhabitants began to leave.

By the time Anse married his intended wife, Ailak, their two families and twelve others were the only people left in the village. The small wooden houses, now abandoned, quickly showed the ravages of the weather. Sheets of tarpaper and skins flapped in the gales and curling boards peeled away from their walls in the wind, which never stopped.

When Ailak became pregnant, she decided to make all new clothing for her husband to show their bond. She worked for months on his *kuilttuk* and *atigi,* inner and outer parkas, new mitts, trousers and boots, out of sealskin she and Ivalu, Anse's grandmother, had prepared.

On October 22 of that year as the arctic night advanced across the dim snowfields and spectral boulders, as the faint green glow of dawn taunted that the total darkness of winter was just ahead, Jago, the young couple's son, was born. Ivalu attended the birth but by evening, Ailak had hemorrhaged and died.

Grandmother Ivalu wept. "It has been so long since I have delivered a child," she said. "So long that I forgot. I forgot to ask leave of Kalupalik the demon over the birth. This is my doing. I forgot!"

Anse said nothing. He had been hearing his grandmother's old superstitions all his life.

Tapeesa, the young wife of old Samik down by the water, had just borne a daughter. She was convinced by Ivalu to be Jago's wet-nurse. The child prospered, though he showed signs of the breathing problems so many children of the village had displayed before him. Anse paid little attention to the child at first, so inconsolable was he at the loss of his wife. Ivalu placed the dead girl's clothes out in the open so that her spirit could escape from them.

In late December, after the total darkness of arctic night fell, an icebound Norwegian whaler spread smallpox through the village. Anse and his son survived. Ivalu, although an old woman, survived, as did Tapeesa and Samik. Everyone else left in the village died. Ivalu said the village had become cursed. She suspected Tupilak, the avenging monster made from parts of many creatures. Anse, by then, had lost the will to disagree with her.

A month before Jago's sixth birthday, his chronic cough and breathing problems got noticeably worse. Anse was worried, as the village had seen this problem for as long as anyone could remember. At least one child died every winter in the village. Ivalu believed her devotionals and prayers had spared her grandson Anse from this malaise. Now she felt she must save her great-grandson.

The old woman prepared tea of black lichen for the boy. When this had no effect, she added the blood of a freshly killed seal to the drink, and made a salve from the seal's fat which she rubbed on the boy's tiny chest.

"I need to find him a doctor," Anse said to his grandmother after the second day of her treatments.

"We have no doctor," the old woman said. "No doctor can appease an angry spirit with medicine. I can give him comfort here until the demon's anger passes."

"It is a waste of time, Grandmother. I must do this quickly. There is a clinic in Illokarfik."

"Two hundred miles away!" Ivalu exclaimed. "Out of the question!"

"Samik's sledge has steel runners. It will move well across the Plain of Annaasak Tarnek."

"The Lost Souls!" The old woman shook her head.

"He has a strong team of dogs. He will let me use them."

Samik quickly agreed to let his friend use his dogs and sledge, although he knew that the younger man was not as skilled in their use as were men of his generation. "Illokarfik is across the great ice plain. Mostly flat," Samik said. "Run the team in fantail formation, not in tandem, two by two. They all feel that they are the leader that way. Carry three weeks' worth of seal meat. Run them 30 kilometers or so in a day. Eighteen miles. Maybe twenty. Some of them are old."

When Jago's condition seemed to improve a little, Anse loaded the sledge with supplies for the trip. He loaded tins of pork, ptarmigan and reindeer meat, tins of pemmican, dried apricots and peaches, his small tent, a bottle of laudanum, his hatchet, a paraffin burner and lamps. His Danish army compass was lost. Samik had borrowed it last year and lost it when his kayak was capsized by a walrus at sea. Anse thought he could navigate by the stars.

Anse made a space at the back of the sledge, near where he would stand, for Jago, lined with furs and blankets. In areas of their route closer to water, they were sure to see bears. Anse packed in his 1895 Winchester and slid his grandfather's ice knife, as long as his forearm and fitted with a walrus ivory handle, into a makeshift scabbard. The moon was waning and circled above, its disappearing light making the snow around him glow almost imperceptibly silver. The dogs would not run in total darkness, Anse thought, the starlight would be all he would have to find their way.

Securing his load with hemp ropes, Anse decided he was ready to depart. A howl arose beyond a rocky hill to the north. The sound was not a wolf howl, but something else. It continued for several seconds, trailing off into what seemed like a woman's wail for mercy. Anse looked in the direction from which he thought the sound had come as hair prickled on the back of his neck. There was nothing to be seen but the snow glow of hills and boulders. Glancing down toward the rocky shore, he saw movement, a faint glow of spectral blue, flickering under the surface of the water. In an instant it was gone, and he thought it must have been a strange reflection of the moon.

Ivalu came out of the house wrapped in fur. Tears on her old cheeks glistened in the moonlight. "I have heard the wailing of Kalupalik," she said. "You must not go. You must not cross the ice under darkness."

"I won't delay any further, Grandmother."

"If you cross the ice, she will find you and claim the boy. I will never see you again."

Samik brought six dogs up to Anse and helped him rig them to the sledge. He said that with steel runners on the sledge, six would be enough. There were three males, Panuk, Silla, and Tonraq, and three females, Nuvau, Uki and K'in. It had been a long time since the dogs had been out in the open, and they could hardly contain their excitement. When everything was ready, Jago, wrapped heavily in furs, came out of the house and took his position at the rear of the cargo bed. "Look in on Grandmother, will you?" Anse said to his old friend.

"Of course we will," Samik said. "Safe travels!"

The trail through the rock outcroppings glowed in the failing moonlight. The energy and enthusiasm of the sled dogs was so extreme that Anse had to continually restrain them. He wanted to get at least twenty miles out of them every day. "Easy, Panuk! Easy, K'in!" he called out to them.

"They aren't used to you, *Ataasek*," Jago said, muffled by his wrappings.

"They learn quickly. In an hour or less they will settle down."

From the rocky shoreline, the land rose though fields of boulders casting shadows in the remaining moonlight across the snow glow. Beyond this, past the summit of a gradual incline, a great plateau opened, stretching to dark mountains in the far distance to the northeast.

The dogs ran, showing no evidence of weariness, for hours. Even so, Anse decided to rest them every few hours and give them strips of seal meat. Jago, in his secure cubby, nibbled on dried apricots now and then, and tried to keep his face covered against the icy wind. His great-grandmother had told him to keep his mouth covered as much as possible and avoid breathing cold air directly into his lungs.

When Anse decided it must be six or seven o'clock in the evening, he decided to make camp. He unhitched the dogs from their leads and they frolicked in the snow until their meals of seal meat were thrown before them. Anse set up the tent and paraffin cooker to heat up tins of pork for himself and his son.

Jago had coughed intermittently all day, but fortunately had no uncontrollable spasms. "How far did we go today?" he asked.

"About twenty miles. Many more to go."

"Why is the doctor so far away?"

"There is nothing left in Tukkat. Not enough people to keep a doctor there."

"Are we always going to live there?" Jago tried to suppress a rumbling cough.

"When Grandmother dies, you and I will go. We will move south to a real town. Tukkat is her home. She will want to be buried there. But nothing will keep us. We will leave."

"Then we will live in a place where there are doctors? And a school?"

"Yes. It's time to get you in school."

Having quickly eaten their evening meal, the dogs huddled together under a slight snow bank to sleep. Jago crawled into the tent and Anse wrapped him tightly in his furs. "I have medicine, laudanum to help you sleep if you don't feel well," Anse said.

The boy shook his head 'no' and immediately fell asleep. Anse removed the Winchester from the sledge and decided to sit up a while with a paraffin lamp nearby.

The sliver of moon was gone. There would be nothing to light the way but starlight and snow glow. A wolf howled to the north. A response came from another direction which Anse could not pinpoint. Like the sound he'd heard before leaving home, it was more like a woman's wail than a howl.

Anse strained to see into the dim distances, but across darkened blue-gray snow fields, among the distant indefinable shapes jutting out onto the Plain of Lost Souls, nothing moved. He checked the lever action of the Winchester. There was a bullet in the chamber. The million stars spread across the sky above him a week ago had multiplied a thousandfold now that the moon was gone. Here, at the limit of the earth, those nights, those vistas, were indistinguishable from drifting in space. This idea first occurred to him as a boy, and it recurred every time he was out in the open during the long night.

Anse removed his pipe from his inner parka and lit it. He thought he would smoke one bowl, then try to sleep. He would watch a while longer to make sure there were no wolves nearby. This plain was said to be an ancient lake frozen over millennia ago. There was no way to know how thick the primeval ice was, having accumulated snowpack and sleet since before the time his ancestors first came to this frozen wasteland.

Anse finished his pipe and tapped it out against the stock of the Winchester. He put out the paraffin lamp and stood. A sudden tremor of the ice near where he stood was accompanied by a crystalline thud from below. Anse steadied himself. To the east he saw a pale blue glow, a spot illuminated from under the ice.

He watched the spot for many minutes. Eventually it faded away to the glazed penumbra it had been before. Anse thought it must have been a whale. Nothing else in the water had the size and power to cause such an impact. If it was a whale then this ancient lake would have to be salt water. He knew that fjords that get cut off from the ocean eventually desalinate. Any liquid water below would have to be fresh now, and if whales lived there, they would have to have adapted. But Anse knew of no breaks or openings in the ice to allow whales to surface and breathe.

Then he remembered a similar blue light off the shoreline back home. The water there was far too shallow to hold the body of a whale or anything larger than a seal. Anse decided to sit up and keep watch until it was time to continue their journey.

Anse let Jago sleep two more hours. He fed the dogs before waking the boy, and the animals were refreshed and full of energy for the day's travelling. Upon rising, Jago began to cough. This grew into a spasm he could not control. He gasped for breath, but every breath he drew in made the coughing worse. After a few minutes, the cough subsided.

Jago had little appetite. Anse wrapped the boy carefully in his cubby and set out. The snow in that region was not deep and the dogs seemed to have the energy to delay their resting times. After seven hours, Anse stopped and made camp. Unleashed, the dogs ate their evening meal ravenously, then playfully attacked and nipped at each other until, in unison, they dug into the snow to sleep.

The next day's travelling was also uneventful. The dogs were still energetic most of the day, but less playful as they settled down to sleep. Anse fed Jago a little and then himself, though he found he could not tolerate much food even though he felt hungry. A *harrumph* sound to the north, Anse recognized as a bear. He thought they must be near the sea. There was little chance the bear would come in their direction, but Anse thought he would sit up until it was time to run again.

The next night at camp, after trying to eat a bit of pork, Jago was seized by another intense coughing fit. Anse held his son tightly until the spasm passed, feeling helpless and unable to give the child anything but emotional comfort. As he held the boy against himself, he noticed something stuffed inside the child's inner parka. Anse removed the object. It was the desiccated body of a ptarmigan with dried grass and leather strips wrapped around it. Anse shook his head in disgust. His grandmother's superstitions. He threw the amulet out onto the snow. Looking further, Anse found a leather strip around the boy's neck. This was tied to a carved walrus ivory *tupilak* or charm, depicting a hideous sea-hag with scales and matted hair. Anse thought of removing this too, but decided to leave it, judging it to be an acceptable gift carved by an old woman for her great-grandson.

The dogs were distressed for a long while by Jago's spasm and coughing. In their uncertainty, they thrashed in the snow and howled. Only after Jago's fit passed did the dogs regain their composure.

Anse let the dogs sleep a few more hours. He thought of the crashing under the ice a few days before. He wasn't sure at the moment how many days ago that had been, but there was no further disturbance since. In the darkness Anse could just make out the face of his pocket watch. It read four AM.

Now was the dark of the moon. He had never travelled before under the dark of the moon. There would be nothing but starlight for the rest of their journey, he remembered. Anse heard snorting sounds in the far distance to the south. Against the dark mountains, an even darker smudge below them must be a herd of caribou beginning their day's wandering, he thought.

The blue glow of the snow fields shown in the dark and stretched in every direction. Anse was sure he had never been this far out on the Plain of Lost Souls. The only other time he had been to the town of Illokarfik, he had gone and returned by boat in summer. He hadn't considered it before, but he was suddenly terrified by the possibility that, like his home village, the town may have died or withered to nothing, isolated as it was on the Arctic Ocean. There may be no clinic or inhabitants anymore. The cold and the darkness easily outwait the depletion of human energies.

When he roused them, the dogs were energetic and strong. Anse thought that what he had heard on the ice days ago would have surely disturbed the dogs if it had been real. He was less sure it had been real. He knew emptiness and desolation can cause the imagination to distort or even create reality. The emptiness of this place, in all directions, cannot defy this. Nearly every man in the village during his boyhood, had stories of spirits or demons terrifying them out on the ice or attempting to drag them to the cold depths of the ocean. It was no life for Jago.

The sky was overcast and the clouds to the northeast looked ominous. A heavy snowfall would slow or even stop their progress. Anse had packed provisions for three weeks. If that ran out, he would have to hunt game for food.

After packing up and running for four hours, Anse stopped the dogs to rest. The dark mountains and hills in every direction looked the same as the ones he had seen when they started. But Anse knew he was not lost. He knew he was still headed toward the northeast winter constellations, even though the deep sky was hidden by clouds now.

As Anse feared, snow began to fall. The flakes were large and feathery: the type that accumulate quickly. He decided to delay the next rest period for the dogs, to get as far as they could in case conditions stopped them. Jago had several minor coughing spells. He'd had no appetite for the dried apricots and pemmican Anse had offered him before they broke camp.

At five o'clock in the afternoon, Anse stopped to make camp again. The snow had tapered off an hour before and the dogs were exhausted. The dogs attacked their evening meal ravenously and, immediately after, curled up against the wind to sleep. Anse had some difficulty opening the tent in the wind, but as the gusts tapered off, he was able to finish the task. Jago nibbled a bit of jerky and then wanted to bed down.

Anse heated up a tin of ptarmigan over the paraffin cooker, and ate it with dried pears. The overcast continued. Since he could not see the stars, Anse thought he might wait to move again until the sky cleared. Without his compass, and after a fresh snow, he was just guessing about his direction.

The snowfall was very slight now. Jago coughed and whimpered a little in his sleep. The snowfall had all but covered the sleeping dogs. Occasionally, one of them would rouse, shake off the snow, and then settle back in to sleep again. After an hour or more, the sky began to clear. The titanic firmament of stars and constellations reappeared over limitless earthly expanses and relit the blue glow of the snowfields.

Anse could see his way now. He looked to the northeast and saw the distant notch of a mountain that he could use as a landmark. He thought he would try to sleep a little next to Jago in the tent. As he stood he thought he saw movement on top of a small rise in the middle distance. He pulled the Winchester from the sledge. He did not know how close they were now to the arctic shoreline. They could have wandered further into the territory of bears. Anse strained to see the rise better in the gloom. He saw a flicker of blue light which jumped from spot to spot, then formed a sort of blue flame. In another second the flame was replaced by a dark form, a black silhouette against the constellations behind it. A howl arose. Anse did not mistake the howl for wolves. It was the howl of desolation, of anger and remorse. The figure was skeletal, appearing to have long, matted hair reaching down almost to the snow. It extended its arms at the crescendo of its wail. The arms were thin, with either tatters of flesh or fabric hanging from them.

A scythe of terror slashed Anse's body. He leveled the Winchester at the figure, but was shaking violently as he fired. The dogs started from their sleep. They shook off the snow and, seeing the distant figure, began barking savagely. The figure moved its arms slowly. The dogs immediately stopped barking and began thrashing around in the snow in uncertainty and fear. They then whimpered and howled, no longer looking in the direction of the apparition.

Anse heard Jago crying in the tent. He looked in at the boy. "Its alright, son," he said. "Just scaring away the caribou. It's nothing." When Anse looked back toward the figure, it was gone.

The dogs soon calmed themselves. Anse crawled into the tent to comfort his son. "How are you feeling?" he asked. "I will get you some food and then we can get moving again."

"Not hungry," the boy whimpered.

Anse touched Jago's face. The child was feverish. "Can't you eat something?" Anse asked.

"No. I'm sick. Too sick."

Anse despaired at the thought of how far they still were from Illokarfik. He quickly packed up the sledge and fed the dogs. In less than fifteen minutes they were on their way again. Their route took them past the spot where the apparition had appeared. The dogs were notably skittish, but obeyed Anse's commands. Anse had covered

Jago's face entirely with a blanket so that none of his skin was exposed as they ran.

After two hours the sky became overcast again. The wind, coming from the southwest, strengthened and snow began to fall. It was a lighter snow than before, but the force of the wind made visibility difficult. Anse ran the dogs for another two hours, he estimated, until they were too exhausted in the drifts to continue.

Anse didn't feel they had come very far, but he could tell the dogs were at their limit. Fortunately the wind died down again and Anse was able to pitch the tent with little difficulty. Jago ate some pemmican and apricots. His fever had not subsided. Anse was too exhausted to sit up tonight. He decided to bed down a while in the tent, then get up and keep watch for a few more hours. He lay next to his son, and lit a paraffin lamp so he could gauge the boy's condition. He felt his son's throat. It was still very warm. "What is this talisman your great-grandmother has tied around your neck?" he asked. He held the object in his hand and examined it.

"She said it is Kalupalik. Have you heard of her?"

"No. My parents...your grandparents would not let her frighten me with her superstitions."

"Kalupalik... is a sea-hag. She steals children and drags them to the bottom of the ocean."

"That is the nonsense of older times. When we move south you will be in school and you will learn about the real world."

Jago was undeterred by his father's dismissal of the story. "She lives under the ice. She is strong there. She can come onto the surface from below through an opening she makes, but out of the water she is weaker. Still strong, but weaker than she is in the sea. She is m...m..."

"Mortal?"

"That's the word. *Mortal.* Or almost mortal. She has to go back into the sea in the place she made to come out. She is a monster."

"Your great-grandmother shouldn't be telling you stories to scare you. I will talk to her when we get home. Of what use is the talisman?"

"You use it to protect me."

"Try to sleep, son. You need your rest."

Anse put out the paraffin lamp. He fell asleep immediately as the sounds of the wind had died down to nothing. Jago slept fitfully. His breathing became labored and he began to cough. Anse awakened. He held his son in his arms until the coughing subsided. The tent shuddered a little and several of the dogs began to whimper out in their snowbank.

The tent shuddered again and in the dim light, Anse saw that something outside was compressing the fabric of the tent. A bulge appeared, then disappeared, only to appear again. Anse had forgotten to remove the Winchester from the sledge. He heard a step in the snow and a whimpering, almost sobbing sound that was not coming from the dogs.

Anse could tell that the dogs, daring not to bark, were paralyzed with terror. The dim starlight was too weak to silhouette the visitor through the tent fabric. Suddenly something crashed against the tent wall behind Jago. Wailing pierced the stillness and sent the dogs into a frenzy of fear. Jago screamed. Anse jumped to his knees and pushed through the tent flaps. He grabbed the Winchester. He turned to face the intruder but there was nothing to be seen.

Jago began to cough violently. "We have to get away!" he cried. "We have to get away from here!"

"It has been following us," Anse said. "Everywhere we go, it is there. We cannot get away. We have to face it here or someplace else." Looking out across the indigo darkness, Anse guessed nearly a foot of snow had fallen. It would be very difficult for the dogs to get through it. They couldn't get very far without resting. If the wind would strengthen, it would create drifts which might make an irregularly passable trail. Anse looked into the tent. "We can't move for a while," he said to Jago. "We can't get through this new snow. We'd need six more dogs to move through this. Are you warm enough?"

Jago nodded 'yes'.

"Can you eat something?"

The boy shook his head 'no.'

Anse scanned the horizon in all directions. After a while he lit the paraffin cooker and ate some pork and peaches. The meal didn't affect his hunger, but he could eat no more. He lit his pipe afterward, took a few puffs, then tapped it out. Noticing a mound in the snow near the trail, Anse brushed it off. It was a granite boulder protruding through the surface of the frozen lake. Under a glaze of ice, there was lichen. Anse chopped at the ice with his ice knife until he could scrape off the lichen. With it, he made tea in a tin cup over the cooker for his son. Jago drank the warm offering gratefully, then tried to sleep.

The dogs huffed and snorted in their snowbank. They were accustomed to long stretches of inactivity on long trips in bad weather. Anse was exhausted. The wind burned his eyes and he wanted nothing more than a warm place to sleep. He scooped snow into his mouth to moisten it. He rubbed snow on his face to revive himself, but his body ached and every joint pained him. He felt that the cold had invaded the core of his body and was slowly freezing its way outward to his trembling skin.

"This was a mistake," Anse thought. If this were summer, he would have found a ship or trawler to take the sea route. But by the time Jago's condition worsened, the ice was just beginning to choke the bays and inlets, so he had considered the overland route his only option. Perhaps his grandmother could have kept the boy stable until conditions cleared. Now, with the storms and whatever horror was pursuing them, they may never make it off the Plain of Lost Souls.

Jago had fallen into a fitful sleep, and coughed intermittently. Anse heard him mumbling something that sounded like "rakeit, rakeit." The boy needed a deep sleep to recover, Anse knew. He found his bottle of laudanum. He awakened the drowsy child and made him sip some of the liquid from the bottle. In a minute, he was deeply asleep again.

The wind picked up anew and started to drift some of the snow toward the southeast. There were five rounds of .405 cartridges in the magazine of the Winchester. Anse dug into his pack and retrieved five more, which he dropped into his pocket. If their progress was halted too many times the seal meat for the dogs would run out and Anse would have to kill a caribou. He hoped their situation didn't come to that. He did not want to leave Jago unprotected while he hunted and dressed out game.

Anse remembered listening to the old men of his village when he was a boy. His grandfather was among them. Many in those days had lived the old life on the ice. They hunted whales and seals and bears. They trapped foxes, they fished. They cut blocks from the ice to build igloos and windbreaks. Many of their friends had lost their lives: killed by bears or wolves, capsized by whales. Some had even starved to death in lean seasons. As time went on, they came to live in the wooden village and find jobs in the mines or on fishing boats. The life didn't suit them, and many turned to whiskey. Then especially they would think of their dead friends and the passing of the old life. They would tell stories of the *Adlivun*, the spirits of the dead, who wander the icy wastes for eternity. They missed their opportunity to leave, Anse thought. They waited until they were too old.

A squalling sound to the north drifted through the mingled sounds of the wind. This sound seemed very familiar, like a bear cub, until it built in power to the wailing and sobbing he had heard before. Anse chambered a round in the Winchester. He squinted into the darkness all around him. The dogs began to whimper and yip tentatively. Anse looked in on Jago. The boy was still sleeping soundly and would, under the influence of the laudanum, for hours.

One of the dogs barked and then burrowed deeper into the snow. Anse raised the Winchester to his shoulder. A hellish scream like tearing metal assaulted him from behind. Before he could turn , talons slashed across his back, ripping through his outer parka. He fell into the snow and, turning, saw a black, spectral figure standing over him. The eyes glowed white and lifeless like the eyes of long dead fish. The face was black, its skin drawn down and folded around a sagging mouth filled with needle-like teeth. The hair was in black strings and knots like seaweed, hanging over an indistinct admixture of black flesh, tattered cloth, scales, and fur. The dead eyes looked at him as the figure began slashing at the tent. It reached inside in an attempt to grab the sleeping boy. Anse by this time had managed to level the Winchester at the figure. He fired. A squeal like a young pig burst from the demon, which seemed to embolden the dogs. They barked and broke out of the snowbank as the figure disappeared into the darkness.

Anse fell against the sledge. He felt light-headed and thought he might pass out. "Back! Back!" he called to the dogs, who had skittered, barking, in the direction the demon had disappeared. Anse chambered another round in the Winchester. "It's weaker," he said, "weaker out on the surface. Grandmother said so. Mortal..."

The slashing of Anse's parka had not pierced his inner clothing. He was not hurt. The side of the tent, however, was severely damaged and would offer much less shelter now. He would try to patch it with an extra blanket. Jago was still asleep. When the dogs returned to their snowbank, Anse fed them. Anse himself, more than anything, wanted to rest, but he knew he would have to stand watch outside indefinitely.

Anse wondered if the creature could go back to the place where it had emerged from the water and revive itself. The ocean would make it strong again. He pulled an extra blanket from his pack on the sledge and threw it over the torn places on the tent. He held this in place with needles made of caribou bone his grandmother always packed for him on his travels. Moving the blanket from the sledge had exposed the hatchet Anse had packed. He decided he might need an extra weapon. He pushed the handle into his wide belt.

Anse's stomach ached. He had not eaten an adequate meal since the journey began. He knew he should have eaten more when he had the chance, but his appetite seemed to disappear as soon as he prepared anything. He was feeling the lack of nutrition now.

The dogs settled down and slept for several hours. Anse lit a paraffin lamp to search for more ammunition in his pack. One of the dogs, Nuvau, a female, sat suddenly upright in the snow and began to growl. She was looking toward the west. Anse looked in that direction and saw a flicker of blue in the middle distance. He fired at where the flicker had been. Nothing. Another dog and another emerged from the snow. They seemed less frightened now. They began barking.

A prolonged scream arose and closed in from the west. At first Anse could see nothing, but soon could make out a black form blotting out the stars behind it. The dogs were suddenly frightened. They barked but spun in circles and would not attack the being. A slashing webbed claw from nowhere shredded the side of the tent again, tearing away the blanket Anse had affixed. Anse fired again as the demon crashed into him, throwing him backward into the snow. The Winchester flew from his hands out into the darkness. The dogs suddenly attacked. They surrounded the demon and tore at its corded flesh and were thrown and struck in defense, in their turn, into the snowbank and against the body of the sledge.

Anse was injured. He tried to stand but couldn't. He felt he had broken ribs and possibly a broken collarbone. He could not retrieve the Winchester. He wasn't sure where it had gone. He drew his long ice knife from its sheath. As the dogs continued their attack, Anse could see that one of the dogs, Uki, he thought, was dead. Another, Silla, lay bloody and injured in the snow. Anse crawled toward the tent. He would defend his son by shielding him with his body.

He thought of the warnings his grandmother had given. He remembered the dead ptarmigan she had hidden on Jago's body. He thought of the talisman she had made and tied around the child's neck. The words Jago had mumbled in his sleep returned clearly to Anse's memory: "Rakeit, rakeit!" This could have been an instruction his grandmother had given in the use of the object. It made no sense. It was gibberish.

As Anse reached his son's side it occurred to him that the mumbled phrase could have been: "Break it!" Had he misheard? He found the leather cord around the sleeping child's neck. He cut it loose with his ice knife. Painfully, Anse backed out of the tent. He crawled to the steel runners of the sledge. He lay the ivory talisman across the runner and, pulling the hatchet from his belt, smashed the object into dozens of splintered pieces.

The demon shrieked in pain as the remaining dogs tore at its throat, face and arms. Tatters of black flesh and liquid sprayed across the snow and the dogs' faces. The black figure wailed pitifully and horrifically and collapsed onto the snowbank as pieces of its form, fingers, ribs, tendons fell away from their moorings.

Anse lay on his back, unsure if he could move. The dogs tore at the crumbling corpse, untempted to eat it, but seemed intent on scattering it in all directions. Anse looked above him at the constellations spinning coldly overhead. He had no idea how injured he truly was. He wasn't sure he was still strong enough to keep himself and his son alive. He didn't know if the remaining dogs could finish the journey. He would have to find the Winchester and try to push on, if he could manage it.

Lying there a while longer, before testing his body's condition, before knowing whether the ice would be vengeful or forgiving, he continued to study the stars, the constellations, the galaxies. Here at the limit of the earth, night was indistinguishable from drifting in space: here, cold and darkness easily outwait the depletion of human energies.

ORIAX OF HELL

NOW I UNDERSTAND MY name, the name given me by my creator. I am Oriax. Oriax of Hell. Sameh said it as he murdered the old teacher who had mocked him so long ago. He named me for a demon of Hell because that is what he intended me to be: his demonic engine of revenge. But I refused to do it.

The old doctor, Doctor Treves, taught Sameh years ago, but mocked his theories and his interest in ancient Arabian medicine. Sameh had always been fascinated by the stories of the blessed saints Damien and Cosmas, Arabians who discovered the elixir called *Opopira Magna*, which allowed them to perform miraculous surgeries to repair broken bodies of the living with components taken from the dead. This elixir was referenced in the ancient tome *Antidotarius Magnus*, which Sameh had found in an old bookshop in Damascus, and studied throughout his youth.

Treves dismissed all this as tribal nonsense and greatly insulted his student, desperate to be taken seriously and shown respect by western physicians, in spite of his desert village upbringing.

Determination abetted by a sense of grievance sustained Sameh through twenty years of research. I am the result of his vindication. In another life, I was a working man. Educated but modest, injured in a terrible accident. Sameh remade me from the limbs and organs of a recently dead giant of a man. I was as an infant. A stranger in a strange land who had to re-learn everything from a nearly void starting point. This process continues. I venerated Sameh as my creator and saw no evil in him nor his intentions until we came to Ste. Odile to find Treves. I could not define evil when I first observed it. I had only a vague sense of *wrongness*, a remnant, I expect, of the man from my earlier life.

The confrontation between teacher and student happened, and was bloody. With Dr. Treves dead and Sameh dying from a gunshot wound in the old doctor's house, I escaped into the night. Now I was truly alone. My protector was dead, having shown me a dark side of himself. The deaths, the violence horrified me, as did my new sense of isolation. I knew my form and countenance were horrific to humanity and that I would surely be blamed for the deaths I had just witnessed. Where would I go? How would I live?

Rouen Street was dark. I heard no sound but the barking of a dog a great distance away. I came to the street called Bosphorous, and looking toward the south, the street seemed to trail off into darkness and wilderness. I crossed a small bridge going out of town. I descended the bank of the creek it spanned, anxious to slake my thirst. The water was salty. A dog closer to me answered the dog barking far away. I thought of how I have always heard dogs barking since I have been aware. Everywhere I have been, at night, across the expanses of this dominion. I thought: they will go mad with barking once they see me.

I passed a small house at the edge of the woodland with a makeshift crucifix displayed in the yard. A long black cloth was draped over the doorframe, signifying, I knew, a recent death within. I pulled the cloth from the nails that held it, and wrapped myself in it. I then continued south on the road into the forest.

The ground became marshy and the vegetation wilder and more fantastic. Off to my left in the darkness, I could make out a small, crude cabin that looked abandoned. I made my way through the weeds and bristles toward it, sinking in mud along the way. The cabin was surrounded by crude implements like a grinding wheel and plow, shovels and mattocks. There was a sizeable pile of firewood that was in an advanced stage of rot. The little house was indeed abandoned. It was one room with a dirt floor. I decided to rest in it overnight.

I tried my best to rest on a cot against a wall. It was much too short for me to lie upon. Sitting up, I slept a little, I think. By morning I was ravenously hungry and in general pain all over my body, as was normal. There were bunches of dried herbs hanging from the ceiling of the shack, but nothing there to eat. I thought I would move to the riverbank nearby in hopes of finding a turtle or recently dead fish in the mud.

I found myself on a spot on the riverbank where I could still see Ste. Odile to the north. I knew there was another town called Belgique to the south, though I had no idea how far. Finding nothing to eat where I stood, I began to move south along the river. There was little food to be had. I caught a frog and several dragonflies, which I ate. I found a dead fish, but it was in an advanced state of decay.

At midday I stopped to rest near a muddy slough. After a moment, I heard hammering atop a hill above me, and the undiscernible sounds of men talking. Climbing up the muddy bank through a cloud of mosquitoes, I saw a small church through the underbrush. It was unpainted and looked newly built. A middle-aged man of moderate height with a slightly portly build was pounding a hand lettered wooden sign into the ground. It read:

CHURCH OF THE HOLIE STEPELKER
PASTOR IS BLESSED REVEREND WADDIE "CUPEYES" BLISS
HELPER IS DEACON ONIE DRATT
COME ONE COME ALL EXCEP FOR CATHLIKS

Another man joined the portly one. This man, Deacon Dratt, as the first man called him, brought a small sledgehammer to Blessed Reverend Bliss. Deacon Dratt held the sign steady while the Blessed Reverend finished pounding it to a stable depth in the ground. I watched them for a few minutes.

Deacon Dratt was very small and thin. His clothes were somewhat tattered and filthy, as were the Blessed Reverend's, but suggested a long-gone prosperity. Deacon Dratt seemed nervous and energetic, while the Blessed Reverend appeared slightly lethargic and methodical. I was very hungry by this time. I decided to hide in the slough until nightfall, in the cloud of mosquitoes, and then see if I could find anything to eat in the vicinity of the church or the two small log homes I saw beyond it.

I covered as much of myself as I could with my black robe. This did little to keep out the mosquitoes as well as the flies that were attracted to my open sutures. I endured this for perhaps ten minutes until I had to throw open my covering for relief. As I did this my arm scraped a dry root protruding from the riverbank, causing it to snap. Glancing toward the top of the bank, I saw the Blessed Reverend and Deacon Dratt looking down at me. Only my head and neck were visible to them from their coign of vantage. "Land o' Goshen, Brother," the Blessed Reverend said. "What happened to you?"

"You was beat by a Ugly Stick," Deacon Dratt said. "Looks like whoever done it just left off, too."

I attempted to respond but only uttered a sort of whimper.

"Come on up here, Brother," the Blessed Reverend said. "If you be outcast, welcome home. " The two men extended their hands to help me climb the bank, but I did it on my own. I stood facing them once I reached the top. I towered over them.

"Dammit all to Hell, I'm glad I didn't run into you after dark," Deacon Dratt exclaimed. "Looks like a plug o' your skull is gone..."

"Calm yourself, Deacon," the Blessed Reverend said. "This right here is a soul who needs kindness and suckher. The Lord has blessed us. We will proceed to give this'un kindness and reckspit, and I believe he can help us here in our crusade. You speak our lingo, Brother?"

"Yes," I mumbled. "Thank you for your help."

"What in God's green earth happened to you?" Deacon Dratt said.

"I was terribly injured. Almost dead. A surgeon, a brilliant man, saved me. Remade me. Reassembled me."

"When did he do this...yestiddy? You look like a hodgepodge of a mess. Like a tornado in the kitchen." Deacon Dratt went on.

"Sounds like the work of the Devil," the Blessed Reverend said. "Satan's work. Are you a work of evil, Brother?"

"No. Of science and skill. My life was *saved.*"

"Well, lookin' you over, I ain't sure how *happy* you ort be about it..." Deacon Dratt put in.

"Enough of that, Deacon!," the Blessed Reverend admonished. "You got a name, my friend?"

"I don't remember my original name. My savior named me Oriax."

"Oriax?" The Blessed Reverend frowned. "Oriax of Hell. The name of the Grand Marquis of Hell. Commander of thirty legions of demons. Well, that there's a hill we gotta climb. But I still b'leeve we can help each other. How about some food, Brother?"

They brought me into the rear of the church into a room where there was a crude table and chairs and a warm stove. The Blessed Reverend directed me to sit at the table. He ladled a plate of something he called dumplings from a pot on the stove and I ate ravenously. Deacon Dratt took a sip of water from a metal cup, and went back outside.

In a moment the door opened again and an old man holding an envelope stepped inside. He was startled to see me, and more so when I stood. "Oh..." he said, with a look of concern on his face. "Good mornin' to you, Eugene," the Blessed Reverend said.

"Whur...whur'd you git 'tis tall drink o' water?" Eugene asked.

"The Lord sent him," the Blessed Reverend said. "The very Lord hisself sent us this lost soul to help spread the word and grow this ministry. This is Oriax. Mangled up in a terrible accident, died, tormented by demons and brought back to us through my ardent prayers and the inference of the Holy Spirit."

"Pleased to meet you, fella," Eugene nodded timidly. "So when did this all happen, Reverend? You been here the whole time."

"*Blessed* Reverend," the pastor admonished. "The title the Lord has give me, as I have told you-uns time and again, is Blessed Reverend. I ain't just Reverend no more nor Cupeyes no more. I put the nickname on the sign to show I'm still one of you-uns, though I have been called by God. You got the widder's tithe there for me?"

"Oh, yessir." Eugene handed the envelope to the Blessed Reverend, who slipped it into his waistcoat. "Head on out now, Brother Eugene. See you on Sunday."

Eugene nodded. He looked at me. "Hope things go a little better for you from now on, Bub." He exited, closing the door behind him.

The Blessed Reverend took my plate and refilled it. "So, my friend, you have nowheres to go?"

"No. My creator is dead."

"Well, here's my preposition. I been preachin' under a tent for two year, but Deacon Dratt and me wanted to put down roots. We just builted this church. We got a congregation, but we can do better. We can draw more people down from Ste. Odile and Lesterton, Oubli, LaMotte, from all over. Tithes will go up and up. You can help us do it. What I just told Eugene...that's our story. I saved you and raised you from the dead. Folks will come from everywhere to see you. So long as you help us out here, you can stay."

I made no response for a long time. The Blessed Reverend's suggestion surprised me in a way I could not quite define. He had lied to Eugene, but perhaps there was no harm in that to serve a greater good. "Yes," I said. "I will help you."

There was another small room in the back of the church which became my quarters. They brought in a cot for me to sleep on, but it was too short, so I slept on the floor. Deacon Dratt built a platform at the front of the church and draped a long curtain in front of it. This was to be my display platform for the Sunday services. I was to be on display.

The Blessed Reverend had handbills printed and he and Deacon Dratt, Eugene and another man, posted them across five or six towns. By Sunday the word had been spread across Ste. Odile County.

The Blessed Reverend kept the front door of the church locked until a few minutes before service was to begin. Before I took my position on my platform, behind my curtain, I could see out one of the rear windows that perhaps two hundred people, a multitude, were waiting to get inside. I felt a great fear and anxiety inside me. I was to be a spectacle for the faithful to gaze upon. I took my place on my platform and waited.

I was wrapped in my black cloak, wearing little under it to have a greater effect upon the congregation. The pain of my body was unrelenting and my wounds continued to seep and attract flies and other insects. Though it was a warm day, I shivered upon my platform. I was terrified at the thought of being a spectacle. I did not know if the fear I felt piercing my body was originating in organs given me from some dead man, or my own. In either instance, my anxiety was real.

When the front door was opened the crowd rushed in. I heard people talking about my shrouded platform as they scrambled to their seats. Some sounded as if they were a few feet from me but none dared to look behind the curtain. I heard footsteps cross the sanctuary in front of me. Then Deacon Dratt spoke. "Friends and neighbors, let's settle down," he said. "The blessings of the Holy Spirit will be upon you today in the form of a miracle. Let's not waste any time. Hear the message delivered to you by the Blessed Reverend Waddie "Cupeyes" Bliss!"

Murmering accompanied the Blessed Reverend's footsteps across the sanctuary. His voice boomed out over the congregation:

"Friends and neighbors? You bet. We also welcome today many new faces, come to see the miracle we have to show and to learn for theirselves that this is the house of truth and grace. We talk about good whupping evil all the time. The Lord Jesus tolt us care for the sick and take in those that need. He hisself casted out demons and raised the dead, but friends, Brothers and Sisters, today I'm gonna show you the word made flesh. Looky here at me raising my arm above my head. How do I do it? Number one, by God's grace, but number two, because I have strength to do it. I have strength to do it because I have food to feed my body, but just verely folks, just verely. After you-uns witness today and see this miracle, we ast that you support this ministry so that the wonder and revelation you will see can be shared with your brothers and sisters in the Lord all acrost this land. If you would deny them that, then Jesus will peg you as nothin' but moochers and layabouts and cry at the thought that you think he don't know how much money you got, and that you don't want to spread the word but only keep it to you own selfish selfs!

"Wait...wait, Brothers and Sisters." The Blessed Reverend continued after a dramatic pause, "I think I done got carried away there. The Lord just nudged me. 'Blessed Reverend,' he said, 'you are my instrument, the key to salvation for my flock here on earth! You and only you! But be patient with my children. Nobody's perfeck!' Therefore, I shouldn't call nobody selfish, but dang it, I get moved by my passion and the importance of what I'm doing here. Let me beg you-un's forgiveness. Can you forgive a man swept up in doing the Lord's work?"

In unison the congregation shouted "Yes, yes we forgive you!" and "Praise God!"

"Now," The Blessed Reverend continued, "I want you-uns to meet a man like you ain't *never* seen. This here is gonna change your life and make you one of our fambly at the Church of the Holie Stepelker. We want you to come back to service every week and support our cause."

"Yessiree," someone shouted. "We'll be here, Blessed Reverend! God love you Blessed Reverend! Show us! Show us!"

I heard the pastor walking toward me. He threw open the curtain. A general gasp swept across the room. Some women shrieked or sobbed, as did many men. A woman fainted and a child in front laughed. The Blessed Reverend pulled off my robe and the reactions continued. "This is the saddest soul you ever laid your eyes on," he said. "Settle down now. Settle down! This is Oriax. Oriax lately of Hell. That's right, Hell."

"Oh good God! Heaven deliver us," I heard from the crowd. I could only look at the floor. I felt ashamed and monstrous. I tried to stifle tears, but failed.

"Friends! Friends!" the Blessed Reverend went on. "Judge not, lessen thee be judged! You-uns have no idear what this poor soul has been through. He is a beacon in troubled times, a blessing upon your own paths, not a old monaster. Oriax, our friend Oriax has been sent from on high. Remember that! He was injured terrible in a accident. They tried to save his life, but he died. Devils of Hell tormented his soul but I prayed over his body and saved him. Through God's grace I brung him back from the dead!"

"Monaster!" a child in front shouted. It was the same one who laughed at my unveiling. He was a boy of about five, of the type doctors call a Mongolian idiot. A middle-aged woman, presumably his mother, stood next to him, and Eugene stood next to her.

The Blessed Reverend smiled. "No, Tector, he ain't no monaster," he said. "He is a miracle. A miracle of faith and the power of the word."

"When did you do this, Blessed Reverend?" an old man called out from the crowd. "You ain't lef' town fer..."

"Doubters will have a harder road to pass than the faithful," the Blessed Reverend interrupted. "But it is my office to forgive all, even rude questions."

"Why didn't God fix him up a little?" another man shouted.

"Who would dare to question the Lord's mysterious ways?" the Blessed Reverend answered. "Now listen here, you-uns. You can come up here closter and get a better look, but don't dawdle too long. And not too many questions. Brother Oriax is tired out and needs to rest."

The congregation quickly crowded around me, nearly stampeding. More than a hundred of them stood, gawking in awe. Some prayed, some wept, some timidly touched my robe. None addressed me directly, but seemed to regard me as an insensate object, a monolith or statue. "Lookit all them weepin' sores," one man said. "He has surely suffered the torments of Hell," a woman added. This continued for nearly an hour. After the people had each taken their turn, they began moving outside to the church grounds to talk about this miracle and question Deacon Dratt and the Blessed Reverend on all the particulars. Children played, men bit off chunks of tobacco or lit their pipes.

Throughout this humiliating pageant, the matronly woman in front and her son Tector had not moved from their seats. When the church had emptied, and Eugene went outside to join the congregation, the woman stood and, taking her son by the hand, approached me. The woman looked me directly in the eye. There was what I would call compassion in her expression. "What you must have suffered!" she said. "I am Elizabeth Saville. The Widow Saville, as they call me here. Can you understand me?"

I looked at her and something in her expression moved me. Little Tector stepped shyly closer to me. Reaching out with his index finger, he touched my leg. "Yes," I said. "I understand you."

"My Lord, dear soul, you're weeping," the Widow said. "What you must have suffered!" She stepped closer to me, studying my face intently. I found I could no longer return her gaze. "I believe you are a miracle made flesh, I do. How else could you have come to us, looking at what you've been through."

"I...am here to serve a purpose," I said, hesitant as I was to mislead her. Tector tried to touch one of my wet sutures, but the Widow brushed his hand away. I wrapped my robe around myself again.

"We don't do that, Tector," she said. "That is impolite." The boy protested and tried to touch me again. "My husband was Swiss," the Widow continued. "He came over here to make his fortune. He did pretty well in dry goods. I was ten years younger, but middle-aged even so. I should have never had a child. My Tector is a change-of-life child. I love him dearly, make no mistake. When my husband died, I felt lost. I didn't know how to be mother to a child who would need lifelong care. I could not abandon him to the orphanage at Ste. Odile. I could not do that. I have been imploring the Lord for strength and guidance ever since. I need His counsel and strength. You are proof that that higher power I seek is real!"

"As you say, Widow," I said. "Anything that gives one comfort must have value."

"I am trusting that the Blessed Reverend is a good man and a true servant of the Lord. I depend upon it. I have given much in tithes to help with this ministry. Now that you are here I know it will grow and the message will spread. You bear witness to the word. That renews my hope!" Tector pulled away from his mother and ran out of the church, drawn, probably, to the sounds of the children playing, which were coming from every direction. "I know this is your resting time, Mr. Oriax. God bless you." She turned and followed her son outside.

I stepped down from my platform. I didn't know if her opinion of the Blessed Reverend was an accurate one. I could not decide whether my answers to her questions were deceptive. I did not want to deceive her. I walked to the near window and looked out on the many people on the grounds. The Widow was talking with a group of women near the riverbank. I saw Tector chasing a group of children who seemed to be running away from him. At one point a boy, slightly taller than Tector stopped and let him catch up. When Tector caught the boy he laughed and embraced him. The boy pushed Tector to the ground. Undeterred, he stood again and continued to chase the other children.

I watched the Widow for a few moments through the church door, speaking to the other ladies. She seemed animated and excited. I wondered if she was speaking to them about me. A child crying drew my attention back to the window. The children Tector had been chasing had pushed him to the ground and surrounded him. One of the boys was pushing grass into his mouth as he wailed and wriggled. As I opened the window to shout at them, Deacon Dratt appeared from behind the church. "Stop that, you dang brats!" he shouted. "You ain't learned nothing from church?" The children ran off in many directions. Tancred sat up, crying, pulling grass and dirt out of his mouth. Deacon Dratt took him by the arm and pulled him roughly to his feet. "You damned little ape! I tolt you to stay away from them kids!"

Dratt dragged the boy by his arm to the church wall just opposite my position inside. I could hear them but not see them. I heard a sound of flesh hitting flesh. Tector cried out loudly, but the general din of the gathering was great enough that nobody heard him. "Yeah, you can't say nothin', can you?" Deacon Dratt went on. "Mumble a couple of words. Stay away from them other kids lessen you want to keep eatin' grass! You let them keep bullyin' you, your ma won't let you out of her sight no more. I won't have it!" I heard the sound of another blow and Tector's crying intensified. I heard Deacon Dratt's footsteps as he walked away. I abandoned the idea of comforting the boy, monstrosity that I am. I doubted I should get involved in the business of the Blessed Reverend or Deacon Dratt. I had nowhere else to go.

The next Sunday the congregation grew. But before the congregation were let into the church and before I took my position on my platform, I was resting in my small sleeping chamber. The Blessed Reverend was having coffee in the adjacent room. I heard the back door open. I recognized Eugene's voice. "Mr. Purviance met with the Widow yestiddy. The paperwork looked real good and he laid it all out for her. Since he's the only lawyer left in Ste. Odile, she is takin' his word for everything."

"Alright then," the Blessed Reverend responded. "I'm gonna see Purviance in the morning to see how its gonna be handled." I heard his chair being pushed back. I pretended to be asleep as his path to the sanctuary took him past my chamber. "Damn!" he whispered as he noticed me lying on the floor. He closed my door.

The church doors were opened. The pews quickly filled and the aisles were crowded with standing people. The Blessed Reverend had sparked interest by promising that I, his miracle, would speak to the crowd. The Widow Saville and Tector were in the same seats they had occupied the previous week. Eugene joined them. The Widow's face was drawn and anxious, very different from her previous aspect. I waited behind my curtain for the Blessed Reverend to appear. An elderly woman began to lead the gathering in the singing of hymns.

The excitement of the congregation seemed even more palpable than the week before. I heard footsteps approaching me. "Dear Mr. Oriax." It was the Widow speaking just above a whisper.

"Yes, Madam. Yes..."

"I am humiliated to bring you my troubles. Much has happened. Things could be falling apart. My comforts may not hold. Such pride in me to have valued them!"

"What is it, Widow?"

"My dear son needs my care so much. He is helpless, nearly mute, but I may not be able to do right by him much longer." I could tell through the curtain that she had begun to cry. "If you can intercede for me in any way with the Lord or heavenly hosts... Mr. Purviance came to see me yesterday. He is a lawyer. He brought papers showing he is acting for the county. My dear late husband! He was so ambitious, so determined to make a good life for me. I knew nothing of this, but it seems he took a loan to get his business started. I thought he had done it on his own with savings. It was a government agency channeled through Ste. Odile County, created to help immigrants start businesses. I saw the documents myself. He could not foresee his early death. The debt was never repaid, and now, with interest owed, it is over $300,000. All I have!" She began sobbing helplessly.

"Widow," I said. "My capacities may not be all you believe they are, but perhaps something can be done. Keep hope. It may be that all is not lost."

The Blessed Reverend Bliss largely repeated his remarks from the previous Sunday. The gathering was most anxious to hear me speak. When the time came, the Blessed Reverend drew back my curtain. The reaction was more pronounced this time than before. The newcomers seemed shocked to find their worst imaginings were correct. It took many minutes for them to quiet. The Blessed Reverend, Deacon Dratt and Eugene all looked at me with expressions I would identify as prideful, or perhaps as satisfaction.

"My dear friends," I began. "It is sorry I am if my appearance has distressed you. It is my burden, my cross. I would change it if I could, but that is impossible. You have come, maybe from great distances, to see me. Here I am. You have seen me. I thought over what I would say to you. The Blessed Reverend counselled me. He said you would want to ask me about God, and Hell and death."

"That's right! That's right!" a man shouted. "Tell us!" said another.

"Let me say to you," I continued, "what is on my mind. I would like to talk about revelations. Not the book in the Bible, but my own. My own revelations."

"We are anxious for testimony, Mr. Oriax," the Blessed Reverend cautioned. *"Testimony!"*

"All I can think of to express," I went on, "is what I have observed. I was not always the same man you see now. I was another man. A simple man but well-read. Then I lost everything. A terrible injury happened and all was darkness."

"You died!" someone shouted.

"I was in darkness."

"And the devils of Hell tormented you."

"'Hell? Why this is Hell, nor am I out of it!' to recall the words of Mephistopheles."

The crowd mumbled in confusion.

"Hell is *here*," I continued. "The Hell of this earth is as bad as any in fable."

"Let's not get too fancy," the Blessed Reverend said. "Let's keep to our message."

"How did the Blessed Reverend resurrect you?" a woman shouted.

"What does the devils look like?" a man called.

"The Blessed Reverend *did* open my eyes," I said. "Since I was first aware I have wondered about the nature of man. I asked my creator many questions on this subject. He nurtured me, cared for me."

"Praise God!" a voice called out.

"He showed me goodness," I continued. "Goodness and love."

"Thank you Lord! Thank you!" Deacon Dratt said.

"This was my experience when I first became aware," I said. "Nurturing, charity and sympathy."

"Doubt not the goodness of the Lord!" the Blessed Reverend said.

"But then I saw something else in my creator," I continued. "There was anger and rage and vengefulness."

"No!" Deacon Dratt protested.

"Yes, yes!" the Blessed Reverend contradicted. "Our God is an angry God, a vengeful and jealous God! A God to fear!"

"I saw other dimensions of him," I said. "I saw that this *man*, this man came to these dark emotions much more easily than to the blessed ones. They were truer to his nature. Then I saw this was true of all men. Nearly all men. I saw this everywhere. Cruelty, deception, violence. My eyes are open now. I am no longer a fool. There is expediency, there is survival. The cost matters little. If the mare struggles to foal only to have the newly born snatched away and devoured by dogs, this is only necessity, not evil. This is only Nature. The way of the world. Kindness is an extravagance. You may, you *should* give it if it does not hinder..."

The Blessed Reverend had signaled Deacon Dratt and they accosted me from two sides and hurried me back to my chamber. The congregation was in shock.

I was exhausted. I sat on my cot and did not protest when they locked me in. Sounds of confusion came from the church. People were shouting and clamoring. I heard someone say "The work of the devils! They still torment him!" I lay on my floor and slept.

I did not rest well. There were still people on the church grounds when I awakened. I sat. Many thoughts were going through my mind. Every moment since my awareness seemed different to me now. A precursor with little value, and to be forgotten. I didn't feel doubt or admiration when I thought of the men scattered across the land. I was not beholden to them, nor fearful, nor inferior. I stood. I pushed the door of my chamber and the doorframe shattered. I was empowered in my perceptions. Looking out the rear room window, I saw Deacon Dratt walking with Tector, holding the child's hand. They were walking in the direction of the garden shed at the rear of the property.

No thought formed in my mind at first. Nature is cruel. Savage, to our minds, but in balance. Suffering is the fulcrum of that balance. But suffering and evil are only separated from reality and objectified in the mind of man. Only men separate it from the daily patterns of life. I watched Deacon Dratt lead the child into the shed. I decided not to resist an impulse that came upon me. I opened the back door and hurried back to the outbuilding.

Deacon Dratt's face went blank when I opened the door. Tector was licking a peppermint stick. Dratt had removed the boy's jacket and shirt. I blocked the door. Tector smiled at me as I put his shirt back on him. I handed him his jacket. "Find your mother," I told him. He tried to put his finger into a wound in my wrist but I pushed his hand away. He stepped out into the dying sunshine and, spotting a rabbit on the lawn, began chasing it.

"You get back in your room!" Deacon Dratt said. "It's no business of yourn. You got a free stay here, You..."

I grasped his throat. He choked and gurgled. A small shears was hanging on the shed wall. Removing it, I gouged out both of Dratt's eyes, leaving them punctured and dangling on his cheeks. He tried to scream, he gasped for breath. With the shears I split his face from forehead to chin. I peeled the flesh back on either side of the cut, then plunged the blades into his brain.

The sense of freedom I felt calmed my emotions. I would find the river and follow the bank south, living as I was able. Whatever I needed I was free to take. Whatever displeased or inhibited me, or threatened to deter my impulses, I was free to destroy. But first, I would wait. I would wait until well past dark. I was anxious again to see the Blessed Reverend.

YOU HATE ME

EUSEBE, I DON'T KNOW why I am the way I am. I don't know how or why I am a person who disgustes you (let's face it), but you do know you can't make a leopard change his stripes? I can't be nobody else. I have tried but people tell me I can't do it. And I don't know what you think of when you think of 'the way I am.'

Little children are curious. Everyone says it and I seen it myself. Many a time. What we done when we was little wasn't nothing. Surely not 'badness'. Just little kids being curious. Is that what this has always been about? Ajax understands. He was in the same sort of trouble when he was a kid. His was worser, though. He got hurted and I think that's why he ain't the man he would like to be. I don't give a care about that. I'm still glad I married him. People has treated him about as bad as they treated me in this life. All you can do is offer it up to Jesus because people is people and you can't make a leopard change his stripes.

You hate me. I know it and always have. I always felt like I disgustes you. You never wanted to be near me, as a kid, nor now. Any time I touched you (always on accident), you would wipe the spot off like I was poison. Like I was something filthy. But I am no more filthier than you. I am not some kind of slimy thing. I am a person.

When I first figured out how you felt about me, about age ten, I guess, I started to notice things. Things about me I decided I didn't like. I was always chubby and clumsy. None of the other girls was. My hair was ugly and some sort of color there ain't no name for. My skin is dried out and splotchy. I would see myself in a mirror and think I didn't look too bad, but then I'd see a Kodak somebody took of me and hate what I saw. And I was always too, too loud.

I got a loud mouth, I know. When kids would laugh at me because I fell, or was fat, or said something stupid that I should of kept to myself, I would cry. I cried very loud and screamed at them even more louder (I come out so much like grandma, didn't I?). All them years of being treated that way, being the laughingstock made me act like that, to cry and scream. It embarrassed you. You said my voice was like metal tearing. They made fun of you for being my brother and all that made you hate me more. They said our family must be the lowest of the low to have something like me in it. If I look at it from your shoes I guess I understand why you was ashamed, but it ain't like I can do nothing about it. No more than those kids would ever stop laughing at me. None of it was ever going to change much.

Maybe. They say anything can happen. I doubt it's true but you got to have hope, I guess. Someday you *might* like Ajax. Someday you *might* like me. Or even love me like a brother should.

Ajax was hit a lot as a kid. Bullied, hit in the face. By other kids and by his uncle who molestered him. He got his nose broke four or five times. That's why it looks that way. Swole and crooked and purple. You can't look at it but you ought to look past it, because he is a good man. He is the only person in the world who loves me and he would do anything I needed him to do.

I always looked up to you, which made all of this worser. I always wanted us to be like normal brother and sister. Ajax admires you too but it hurts him that I do, and that you are so put off by me.

Maybe being closer could never happen because our family wasn't normal. There was something wrong with us. You said once, we was 'diseased'. I don't really know what you meant by it but I know you know what you're talking about.

You were always so smart, and a good-looking man. I don't know why you have so much trouble with the women. I think they must all be crazy. They should be glad to have you. That's my opinion, at least. You think that diseased part ruins everything for you. You would know better than me. You know so many things that I don't. What happened with Oscar was proof.

That mean old goose, Oscar. Nobody knew where he come from. Everybody said he was always around our pond for as long as anyone could remember. So mean and tough. He killed a fox once. Actually killed a fox. Uncle Walter said "I bet you could cook that bird for a week and still couldn't stick a fork in the gravy." I didn't get it at first but when I did I laughed so hard! Ajax loved him, though. Loved that mean old bird. Ajax would sit on the stump and feed him corn and worms and leftovers. Oscar would take the food, then bite Ajax, but Ajax always gave him more food. He knew old Oscar couldn't help being mean. An old bird don't know no better.

You didn't care for Oscar. You like animals and you like learning about nature, but he bit you when you brung papers over for me to sign. Since then you was screamish around him. It was Ajax got the idea. Like I said, he loved the bird but he knowed how important it was to me and to hisself too, to have you like us. He figured a sacrifice had to be made. In the days of the Bible the Chosen People had to sacrifice something they loved to please the Lord. Reverend Bliss told us that and Ajax understood.

That Christmas morning he started working on his surprise. Ajax brung out a bag of peanuts and spread them on the oak stump. Oscar come running. The old bird bit Ajax a half a dozen times, and then he started pecking away at the peanuts. After a minute of Oscar enjoying hisself, Ajax brung down the cleaver on him and cut off that hard old head.

The old bird's head rolled off the stump and onto the ground. Ajax said it looked like the head knowed something was wrong, laying there in the snow for a few seconds, then figured out it was the end and accepted it just before it went glassy-eyed. The headless body flopped around spraying blood everywhere, like in a fit to know what just happened to it.

Ajax broke down bawling to see all that, to think he did such a thing to his old friend. I plucked the body clean and washed it off. Then I put it in the Dutch oven so we could bring it over to you.

I'm stronger than Ajax but I knew I couldn't carry that heavy carcass all the way to your place, especially in the cold. We put the Dutch oven and Oscar in the wheelbarr and started off to your house through the snow.

I didn't plan that we should eat with you. I knew you wouldn't want that. I am at least smart enough to know you hate me and you can't stand the look of Ajax's face. I was just going to cook the bird for you at your house, make the stuffing and giblets and such on the spot so's it would be fresh and hot, and then we'd leave. You could enjoy your Christmas meal in peace. Our holiday surprise for you.

No sooner do I lug the Dutch oven inside your kitchen than you pitch a fit. "What are you bringing in here?" you said.

"Christmas dinner for you," I said. "Old Oscar won't vex you no more. He had his day of being a nuisance. Ajax'll miss him but he'll make a good meal for you. Merry Christmas, my brother!"

"What made you think I would want to eat that filthy old goose?"

As many times as you have looked at me so disgusted, so put-off, I was still surprised at how you looked at me then. I never felt so low nor so stupid. "Well, I thought..." I was sputtering.

"He ate garbage and carrion and...shit! Get it out of here!"

"But," I said, "all animals do that, don't they? If you ever notice what them hogs eat! Land o' Goshen!"

"Get out!"

I looked at Ajax and he had tears in his eyes. He always been a man who feels things in a big way. He cries a lot. At that moment I was too. Crying. It was nothing left to do but put the old bird back in the wheelbarr and come home.

So that's what we done. We didn't say much on the cold walk. I didn't know if I should bring up the subjeck of us eating Oscar our own selves. I thought we could give the bird to a poor family, but I didn't know of any, and I was wore out and freezing from all that walking in the snow.

But if we didn't eat the bird, we would have to throw it out, which seemed like such a waste to me. We ain't rich neither. But then again, Ajax was just bawling and carrying on to beat the band, so I didn't say nothing.

Ajax's busted up nose runs like a spigot in cold weather. Add all his crying to that and it is a sight to see. When we finally got home, Ajax run to the tool shed and got a shovel. I had been pushing the wheelbarr and he told me to stop at a spot beside the house. He started to try to dig in that frozen ground to make a grave. I just let him be and went on inside.

He was outside almost two hours, I would say. When he come in he was froze through. His face was all red and fleckered with frost. His eyes and upper lip was crustered-up with froze tears and mucus. He set on the davinet with his coat and scarves still on. "I been thinkin'," he said. "You allus wanted your brother to love you."

I shrugged. I was ashamed at what he said, but he hit the nail on the head, that's for sure. "I don't know why it means so much to me," I admitted. "But it does. Yes."

"I done killed Oscar for nothin'. It was for nothin' if we just give up and let it go at that."

"My brother thinks we're sick in the head. I don't know what to do. I wisht I could let it go."

"If we lets it go, Oscar died for nothin'. I know what to do, but we got to do it *now!*"

I didn't think I would make that cold walk again in the same day, but I did. My feet was numb and my face burning from the cold. The walk seemed twict as far as it had been that morning. But I had my thoughts to keep me going. I kept thinking: "this will be the thing that does it! Nobody that has got any love in them could just throw us in the garbage after doing something like this. No greater love, as the Good Book says."

As I got closter to your house, though, I had some second thoughts. I mulled them over and over again, and by the time I got to your back porch I had drove them out. I had no doubts anymore. Your housekeeper let me in the kitchen door. She said you was in the parlor.

You looked put-out and angry to see me again. "What do you want now?" It was more of a bark than a statement. "You left Ajax at home this time?"

"I did. Yes, I did," I said. "He ain't well. Took to his bed. He won't be hisself for a few days."

"What's the matter with him?"

"He fell sick after we got this idea for you."

"What idea?"

Out of my pocket I took the linen cloth. Wrapped again and again as it was, discolored brown and soaked with the clear and the red lixer of life. I handed it to you but you wouldn't take it. You kind of froze as I laid your newspaper acrosst your lap and pulled the linen wrapping loose. The twisted nose was brown and purple and seeping them fluids. Now you could see for yourself what we would do to please you. You swept the bloody thing off onto the floor. You coughed and retched a little. *"Get out of here!"* Your face was so red and so raged. "Never come back. *NEVER!*"

I said nothing. I couldn't think of nothing to say. Nor nothing more to do. Ajax needed care. I needed to treat his wound. He done it for nothing.

I sat on the porch step and thought of you, my brother. I thought of how I'll never know for sure why I disgustes you like I do. Family should never be like this, that I do know. And I know that whatever you call this situation, I can never fix it. I sobbed a little just then and thought: "You hate me."

THE ORIGIN OF
THE WORLD

THE ROAD PAST ST. MATHURIN'S Asylum may as well have been a dead end. It was all but unused by anyone in Ste. Odile who had no business to conduct at the place, the place that caused Pettibone to weep when he first laid eyes on it. The asylum.

St. Mathurin's was an expedient used by families at a tragic moment, then urgently forgotten. It was so far from town, so lost in the hills, it was easy to forget, and that was a comfort. Pettibone saw it as a failure. It was the final proof that he would never make anything of his life.

He had planned his future. By the time he entered Carthesian University, he'd put his disgrace behind him. He convinced himself that his behavior then was not his true nature, and his father had paid the families for their silence. As he entered college, it was as if those things had never happened.

He was abnormally tall, and thin as a sandstone spire in the desert. His hair had begun falling out in his adolescence, caused by his 'nervous nature,' the family doctor said. He became an object of curiosity as he grew older, attracting unwanted attention wherever he went. He was embarrassed and humiliated by this. He wanted to lose himself in learning and research.

He would be a chemist. He'd started reading about efforts to create a purine derivative to forestall tissue rejections in transplants while still in prep school. As he got older he became more interested in other pharmacological research, particularly as regards diseases of the thyroid. But he could never fully purge his mind or impulses and clear his thinking.

Females are the origin of the world. He could not completely erase that idea from his mind. All things begin with them, are nurtured and grow, are saved or rejected through them. *L'Origine du monde,* as his new friend De Lancre termed it. All passions and desires corroding his sensibilities lived in them. Mature women, the sows, yes, but more the young ones, the girls who knew nothing of this brutal life. Only these could be mastered. The mature ones, the ones who know, have their wantonness and caprice to control weak men.

He left Carthesian with his degree incomplete after assaulting one of his professors over the ineffectiveness of his protocols. The offer of a laboratory position at Osage Lead in Ste. Odile brought him to the forgotten village on the Mississippi. He was made supervisor of the ore assay laboratory, work which he quickly found to be monotonous and unrewarding.

Pettibone's temperament and proclivities soon drew him to company with similar inclinations. Office holders in town government, company presidents, and even a judge all became Pettibone's familiars. He expected to find the friendships useful. One evening after a Knights of Pythias lodge meeting, Dr. Guildea of St. Mathurin's asked Pettibone if he was happy with his position at the laboratory. "Tedium weighs on me," Pettibone said. "That, and the stupidity of those I have to work with, is too much. I dread each day. My hair has started falling out faster...from my nervousness, I'm sure. That, with my height, makes me a spectacle, an object of curiosity."

"I could see you were distracted," said Guildea. standing. He stood over Pettibone, still sitting in his lodge chair. He examined Pettibone's scalp. "What you have here is what Hippocrates called alopecia. Hair loss. It's a disease, not nervousness."

"Is it? I think I have heard of it."

"You dislike working with the stupid. I wonder if you could abide the insane?"

"At St. Mathurin's? Are you offering me a position?"

"Yes. I need someone to run the facility, someone with more vigor than I have. It's become too much for me and leaves me no time for the publishing I want to do. I cannot say if it would suit you or not. I think you are very capable. You know how to manage people. I think you are a man who will do what needs to be done in a position like this one."

"Very possibly." A smile crept across Pettibone's pale face. "Observing the insane, learning about the causes and cures for mania would be fascinating. The insane don't choose to be so. The stupid, in my estimation, often do."

Even the inmates at St. Mathurin's, both in the male and female wings, seemed to look at Pettibone as an oddity. Pettibone had never actually seen the building before the day he assumed his responsibilities. Its dilapidated state shocked him and caused him to doubt whether this career change had been an upward move or not. As Dr. Guildea escorted Pettibone through the gray corridors to his office, the inmates watched him with suspicion, curiosity and fear. Howling and screaming could be heard coming from one end of the hallway to the other and from the floor above. An old woman stood naked in the doorway of a ward, staring blankly at something visible only to her on the opposite wall. A young woman ran past, chased by another, playing some sort of game together. "Do not run in the hallways, Lena! Marie!" Guildea called after them. "This is the women's ward. Your office will be here." Guildea unlocked a door in an alcove, the top half of which was translucent glass. The office was of a moderate size with one window. It had obviously not been used for a long time.

"This will do," Pettibone said.

"I will begin sending over the case files and dossiers and when you are settled, we will schedule a time to go over them and discuss care of problem patients," Guildea said. "We also have some personnel issues. Several positions to fill."

"Very well, Doctor. This is the women's ward?"

"Yes. The men are at the opposite end, first and second floor."

"I think I will be just fine here."

Pettibone and Guildea spent most of Pettibone's first week at the facility discussing theories of various manias and treatment policies and resident patients showing those symptoms. It soon became apparent to Pettibone, and obvious to Guildea, that of all the varieties of madness to be observed in the asylum, the new superintendent had a particular interest in female sexual hysteria, especially as found in younger girls. "This is a serious profession, my friend, and our mission a medical and humanitarian one...this is not a confectioner's shop," Guildea admonished.

Pettibone took the insult with a smile. "You misunderstand me, Doctor."

"I have every hope that is so."

Every morning when Pettibone arrived at the asylum, he walked the hallways among the inmates from one end of the building to the other. He did this imperiously, condescendingly, drifting through their stink, so that the patients could adjust themselves to his dominance over them. The men often ignored him or avoided eye-contact. The women seemed both more curious and more fearful. Several of the young women, and a few of the older ones, looked at him coquettishly, smiling slyly or giggling. Some even bared their breasts or legs, but he made no response to this. They were filthy creatures, but held much fascination. Everything began and ended in those fetid regions, rank and impure as they were. They were the origin of the world.

When he would return to his office after his morning walk, he would think of the feral figures giggling and screaming and writhing outside along the hallway. It is right, he thought, that women pay the eternal price for their sins against man. It is a legacy of depravity, a debt that can never be repaid. It left a world that cannot be made right and pure again. It throttled innocence out of human experience, except as a fleeting condition or an ideal that can rarely be attained. Yes, innocence is but a fleeting condition at best. Pettibone found that this fact enraged him. Women, in all their aspects, were nearly always on his mind.

As good as his word, Guildea left Pettibone to his own devices. Pettibone's lodge brothers were curious about his new position and his new duties. Only when Guildea missed a monthly meeting of the Knights of Pythias did Pettibone feel free to talk about them in a more casual way.

"You must feel surrounded by them," Evers the pharmacist said. Four of the lodge brothers were sitting near the fireplace after the meeting had ended. "I would feel...outnumbered, I suppose."

"No great beauties among them, I'll wager," Mitchell said.

"After a good scrubbing there are two or three who might surprise you," Pettibone smiled. He removed his pipe from his frock coat pocket and lit it with one of the matches he always carried.

Mitchell laughed. "Clean a couple of them up and let's have a look!"

"It's an idea, isn't it?" Pettibone said. "It occurred to me that I could put their idleness to good use."

"Are you thinking of renting them out?" De Lancre asked, glancing at each of his lodge brothers.

Pettibone shrugged. "That wasn't what I meant...necessarily. I was thinking more of giving them legitimate skills that could earn money. Money for the asylum."

"I think that's what we are talking about too!" Mitchell laughed.

"No, I mean they could do things like sewing, laundry, chemical dry cleaning, leatherwork," Pettibone went on. "There are twenty or so of them who are capable of such work. And at some moment in the future, I could expand their duties into...other areas."

"You would have to convince Guildea," De Lancre said.

"Whatever I do." Pettibone stood, towering over the company, and pushed a log into the fire with his foot. "Whatever I do, I am not sure Guildea would even notice."

Pettibone presented his invoices to Guildea for mops, brooms, feather dusters and other housecleaning supplies, and Guildea signed them all without reading them. Pettibone had contracted with the Lamarck Hotel in Ste. Odile to provide maids and other staff from the ranks of St. Mathurin's more cogent female inmates. Six women were selected, and they seemed excited to leave the asylum for eight hours every day, accompanied by two guards, even if they had manual work to do. The women enjoyed being occupied, Pettibone noticed, and by creating two separate sets of receipts for the job, he was able to keep a twenty percent profit for himself.

On a Friday morning Pettibone sat at his desk organizing his inflated receipts and storing them in a strongbox. A tapping on his door frame startled him. "I am sorry to bother you, Superintendent." It was Esther Ridgeway, a patient in her late thirties who had killed her husband defending herself against his beatings.

"Esther! I wasn't expecting anyone." Pettibone seemed embarrassed he had reacted as he did. "Yes? What do you need?"

"Well, Superintendent, I want to help out. I want to do things that help you out, you know? And the asylum. I want to help out the asylum too." She stared awkwardly at the floor. "I can do a job. Any job you say. I want to help you out as superintendent."

"Oh yes?"

"I could do maid work, or anything." She glanced at Pettibone furtively, as though ashamed of an aching in her she was incapable of masking.

"Can you now?" Pettibone smiled. "Do you know what dry-cleaning is?"

"No sir."

"It's cleaning garments with chemicals instead of water. No one in town does it. We will be first."

"Yes sir. That's good...sir."

"I am a chemist by training. Naptha, aromatics, ketones and others may be used to remove stains and soil from garments that could be ruined by water."

"I am sure I could do that, Superintendent."

"There is an odor and vapors to deal with, from the solvents. I am going to set up shop in the old brick garden shed at the edge of the property."

"Good use for it, I would say. Home for rats and spiders now."

"Meet me at the shed tomorrow at ten am. We will discuss it. I will give you leave through the floor supervisor."

"Oh yes, sir!" Esther's face brightened. "If you are coming in on a Saturday I know it is important to you, sir!"

The old garden shed was in a state of near collapse. The mortar holding the bricks together had long-since deteriorated to a sandy compress easily eroded by the touch of a finger. The roof was warping metal and at the northeast corner, rotted and rusted away and open to the sky. As Pettibone walked the flagstone path to the shed, he saw Esther waiting for him at the front door. "Here I am, Superintendent," she said. "Right on time like I told you."

"So you are, Esther." Pettibone pulled open the splintering wooden door. The inside of the building still housed a few garden tools, a wheelbarrow, potting tables and cracked pots with long-dead plants in them. All was covered in dust and draped in cobwebs. One window was placed in the north and one in the east wall. The glass panes were intact. A scuttling sound under one of the potting tables startled Esther. A rat ran from the shadows and out the open door.

"Such a mess!" Esther said.

"I will leave it up to you to clean this up," Pettibone responded.

"Yes Superintendent. I will do my best."

"I will assign you a helper. We will get one of your floor mates to help you here."

"Artemesia would be good, Superintendent."

"Yes, I have noticed her. Very young. Thirteen, if I remember right. Will she work?"

"Twelve. I believe she will. I have taken her under my wing."

"Semi-catatonic, as I remember. I hope she has the energy. She is your responsibility."

"I can fetch her now, if you wish..."

"No, not now." Pettibone pushed the shed door closed. "You seem very lightly dressed today Esther. Thinly dressed."

Esther looked timidly at the floor. "Am I, Superintendent?"

"You know this, of course." Pettibone reached for an old tomato stake leaning against a potting table. With it he lifted the bottom edge of Esther's shift. He lifted the fabric as high as Esther's upper thigh. There were no undergarments. "I could see the sloshing and bobbling under your dress, of course, as you intended. Your file says you are forbidden to wander into the men's wing."

"We all are. All women are forbidden. As are the men. Vice versa."

"But *you* especially. A note says to keep an especial eye on you."

"Well, sir, I don't know... God gave women certain curiosity and...need."

"Do you know that you stink, Esther? Hair, mouth and body."

Esther flushed with humiliation. "I am so sorry, Superintendent. I tried to clean myself but we can only bathe once a week, and then we are only given a few minutes."

Pettibone dropped the tomato stake and replaced it on her thigh with his hand. "Be still. Close your mouth. You are only as you were conceived by Jehovah. An allurement. A temptation. As you present yourself to me now, you are as you are intended to be. Stinking, filthy, dark and deep. Accessible or maybe inaccessible. Ever more repellent in your aging. Your depth is. Your secret is. It's there...that is the origin of the world."

Pettibone wondered why he had not taken more notice of Artemesia before. The girl trailed behind Esther out to the garden shed every morning, at first to help clean it out, then to set up the dry-cleaning facility. She was a slender girl, beautiful as a melancholy Pre-Raphaelite heroine, and looked younger than her twelve years. Pettibone noticed that her hips were just beginning to widen, and knew that puberty would soon overtake her childish demeanor. She had come to St. Mathurin's a year ago. She was unable to speak clearly and she had set fire to her neighbor's chicken coop. She was an earnest and diligent worker and seemed a perfect helper for Esther in the new enterprise.

The morning that the cleaning solvents arrived, Pettibone decided to look in on the progress at the shed. McVie, a carpenter Pettibone had hired in town, was finishing an annex building meant to house a wood-burning stove.

The interior of the shed was tidy and well-swept. The space now looked surprisingly big to Pettibone. Artemesia was helping Esther lift large glass jugs of solvents into cradles McVie had made for them, on one of the tabletops. Esther's face brightened when she saw Pettibone. "Almost ready here, Superintendent! We're doing a real good job, I think you'll agree."

Pettibone looked at her coldly. "Yes, very good work. I see you have put your helper to good use." Artemesia looked at Pettibone shyly. "What did you do with all the rubbish in here?"

"We throwed it in the woods, out back." Esther saw she was not going to coax a smile out of Pettibone. "We're doing our best. Yes, Artemesia has been a big help."

"Good. I am very glad to hear it." Pettibone smiled at the young girl and she blushed and looked away. "I knew she would be a good choice."

"Why are we putting the stove separate from this room? We need it handy to keep the irons hot." Esther pushed a glass jug into its cradle.

"These jugs hold cleaning chemicals," Pettibone said. "Solvents. Naptha, toluene, methyl ethyl ketone. Aromatics, aliphatics and ketones. Very volatile. The vapors will ignite in the presence of an open flame."

"But we have to go outside to get to the stove," Esther protested.

"It's safer to have no connection, no door that vapors can seep under. That is why McVie built a wide shelf inside this adjoining window. When you retrieve the hot irons, place them on this shelf so you do not have to carry them outside around the building and they don't cool off when you do. Place them there on a rack and retrieve them when you are back inside."

"But we won't have any warmth in here in the wintertime," Esther said.

"All the more reason to keep busy," Pettibone answered.

"Superintendent Pettibone." McVie stood in the doorway. "I need to go to Luke's for more nails."

"Did you get the stove offloaded from the wagon?"

"Yes sir. It's on the drive along with the flue. I'll need a cart to bring it down here."

"You should have left it on the wagon and driven it down."

"Dr. Guildea said no."

"Did he?" Pettibone smiled. "Artemesia, go fetch the flue and piping and bring them down to the shed while Mr. McVie goes to town." Artemesia nodded and rushed out the shed door.

Esther glanced furtively at Pettibone. A coy expression faded as soon as he returned her gaze. "Superintendent," she said. "I wanted you to know I am available any time. Any time you say. What we did was a good thing. A good thing for me. I was willing. It wasn't forceful. I was willing and I am again."

Pettibone lifted a jug labeled 'Toluene' onto the tabletop. "Esther," he said, "how dare you bring up such a subject."

Esther's face went blank. "Well, I just meant..."

"You forget yourself. I do not expect you to do that again. You are suggesting something unethical and improper for a man in my position."

"I didn't mean..."

"Do you ever clean your teeth, Esther?"

"Well, no. We aren't given any..."

"Everything stinks from your mouth to your dark regions. I smell you from here. Please direct your face away from me when you speak. Do you imagine I would seek some sort of intimate congress with you?"

Tears began to form in Esther's eyes. "You... did before."

"You are withering away. You should see yourself in this sunlight. Wrinkled, corrupted, desiccated. If I should ever stoop so low as to require a secret moment with you, if I ever wish to debase myself to that low strata, I will tell you. But you are never to mention it. Never in your remaining days on earth, or you will wish you had another filthy garderobe, other than this one, in which to rot away the rest of your life."

Esther burst into tears. She ran out the shed door and back toward the tree line of the hardwood and cedar forest.

Pettibone placed the remaining solvent jugs in their racks. As he did he toppled a whiskey bottle which Esther had washed out and filled with toluene to spot-clean fabric. The vapors made Pettibone's face flush and he felt light-headed. He stuffed a cleaning rag into the opening, stumbled to the door, and set the bottle outside on the ground. The vapors were overwhelming inside the shed. Pettibone stepped out again and decided to stay outside until the vapor dissipated.

He saw Artemesia struggling down the hillside with the flue and piping for the stove. He looked toward the woods but saw no sign of Esther. It occurred to him that Esther had killed a man. She was capable of murder. He would keep his guard up in her presence from now on.

Pettibone thought about lighting his pipe, but instead he walked up the hill to help Artemesia. "I'll help you with those," Pettibone called as he approached. "Too much for a young girl to handle." He took the flue from her and she nodded, blank-faced, in appreciation.

At the bottom of the hill, Pettibone laid his burden on the ground outside the annex. Artemesia did the same. "Leave these out of McVie's way until he is ready for them. Step inside here with me, girl." Pettibone entered the shed and Artemesia tentatively did as she was told. "I am sorry about the smell," Pettibone continued. "Solvent spilled. I know you can't speak well, which must make you a better listener." He leaned against a table as the girl stood motionless in the middle of the floor. "You are wondering where Esther has gone. She ran off into the woods. I haven't seen her since."

Artemesia frowned and looked at the open door. Pettibone thought the girl might bolt out of the shed, but she stood still. "You look concerned, Artemesia. You don't need to be," he said. He moved closer to her but leaned against the wall when a fearful expression overtook her. "You have nothing to fear," Pettibone continued. "Why would you? You are so young. You haven't yet seen all there is in the world that should rightly cause you to fear. Here you are safe. With me you are safe. Everything that comes into being rots away. Living things, certainly, but everything else, too. As soon as you were born, you began to decay. Slowly at first, but inevitably. It's an ugly process. It has yet hardly touched you. When you see it around you, a crippled old dog, rotting crops in a field, an old woman bowlegged and hunchbacked, struggling up her stairs, you remember this is the slow process of dying."

Artemesia stared at Pettibone in complete confusion. She glanced toward the open door. Tears had begun welling in her eyes. "That old woman," Pettibone went on, "is probably a widow, having pointlessly outlived her husband. The allure of any purity she ever had is gone. She is useless in old age. A burden. Her home is by now infested with roaches and ants because she can no longer keep a house. There is no longer a tooth in her wizened skull, her mementos are covered in dust, and her body stinks. You will be there someday, my girl, an object of revulsion."

Artemesia could no longer meet Pettibone's gaze. She stared meekly at the floor. "But you are not there yet," Pettibone continued. "The old woman struggling up the stairs...do you know why she is a widow?"

Artemesia shook her head 'no.' She sniffed as tears tricked down both cheeks.

"That would be," Pettibone went on, "because her husband did dangerous, life-shortening work throughout his life to support her and her children. He may have been a miner suffocating in coal dust, or a sand-hog sunk in a caisson underwater building a bridge, or a foundry worker inhaling fire and toxins. It was his lot in life: to give himself up for them and to die early. The tiny male mantis mates with the larger female. His main purpose completed, he then becomes merely a source of protein to strengthen her, and fortify her eggs... and she devours him. Just as women devour men. They sap their vitality and life blood, like vampires. This is as Nature decrees. Every man knows this on some level, and our defensive response, futile as it is, is to dominate you. But in the end we dissolve into irrelevance because in you is the origin of everything. The world."

Pettibone stood to his full, imposing height. Artemesia was sobbing audibly now, and trembling in terror and confusion. Pettibone approached her. He reached out and touched her shoulder. She whimpered and pulled away from him. "Why are you crying?" Pettibone said "Too much ugliness for you? Don't be foolish, girl. The world is an ugly place." He reached out to stroke her hair, but withdrew his hand. "I am offering you the opportunity to use what you have now, before that ugliness happens. The laws of Nature are not my doing. You should use to full advantage the purity you still have, that which powerful men who can protect you desire. You would be clever to use it before it is gone and you become old and repellent."

Esther suddenly stormed through the open door. She pushed Artemisia roughly aside. She looked at Pettibone murderously. "This is what you're after, is it?" She spat out the words. "I listened. I listened to you from outside."

"Nothing I say or do privately is any of your concern." Pettibone looked at his accuser disdainfully. "What I do I will do freely and you will say nothing and mind your own affairs. If I chose to have her right here in front of you, there is nothing you could do about it. Remember the power I have over you and remember you are alone in the world." He smiled broadly. *"Crabbed age and youth cannot live together..."*

"I ain't a crab age!" Esther said. "If you mean old. I ain't old yet!"

Pettibone looked goatishly at Artemesia. "She is a naiad of the mongrel class," he said. "Finish your work in here tonight. Tomorrow, if Mr. McVie finishes, we will begin the dry-cleaning." He stepped outside and closed the shed door.

Pettibone stood for a moment, looking up the hill at the gray edifice of the asylum. He removed his pipe from his frock coat pocket and lit it. It was late afternoon. He would be going home to his rooms at Tranquille House in town soon. He thought he would have his dinner at Herve's, the closest thing in Ste. Odile he had found to a fine restaurant.

McVie had still not returned from town. Pettibone assumed he would smell liquor on his breath when he came back. The sound of Esther's angry voice arose from the stillness inside the shed. "It's sickness," she said, *"sickness* in him to lust after a child!" Pettibone smiled a slight smile. "Once he starts you whorin' at twelve, that will be your whole life!" she continued. "You won't refuse, will you? *Will you?"* The crash of breaking glass startled Pettibone. He rushed back into the shed.

Artemesia lay on the floor partially under a table, in a pool of her own blood. The child's foot twitched a few times and a pink bubble bloomed from the gash in her throat and popped. She lay still.

A broken glass shard was still in Esther's hand. She dropped it. "Good enough for her," she said, as if in a trance. "I saved her...from *you!"*

Pettibone was blind with rage. He smashed his fist into Esther's face and she collapsed limply onto the floor. She lay in a heap next to the solvent table. Her jaw had been displaced. Pettibone could see that her condylar processes had been broken and forced out of their sockets and now were positioned behind her ears. But she was alive. Her breath gurgled in her throat repulsively. Behind him one last gasp of air bubbled from Artemesia's throat. Esther drew a semi-conscious breath.

His rage refreshed, Pettibone lifted the jug of toluene from its cradle. He removed the cap and forced the neck into Esther's shattered mouth. Esther spat and choked as the fiery liquid flooded her mouth. She sprayed it out past her limp jaw and screamed a muffled scream as it made its way down her throat. Pettibone covered the edges of her mouth with his hand so the solvent could not escape. Esther's body heaved and a spray of vomit and toluene spattered Pettibone's coat sleeves. Then, glassy-eyed, she lay still.

Pettibone stood upright. He dropped the jug on the floor and it smashed to pieces. The room filled with the hallucinogenic vapors. He removed his frock coat. He retrieved his pipe and matches from a pocket, and dropped the coat on the floor. He hurried outside.

With his elbow, Pettibone smashed a pane in the west window. Picking up the whiskey bottle he had dropped before, he struck a match to the rag he had stoppered it with and threw the bottle into the window. Flame bloomed enormously inside the room and in seconds all was engulfed. Pettibone stepped back up the hillside. He watched the fire burn until he was certain the charred bodies inside were useless in any possible investigation.

Pettibone suddenly realized that McVie was standing next to him, and that the hillside above was lined with the asylum's inmates, staff and Dr. Guildea, watching the conflagration.

Dr. Guildea gave Pettibone a few days leave of absence to recover from the trauma of trying to rescue the two victims of the terrible accident. When he returned to St. Mathurin's that Thursday, he went immediately to Guildea's office. "Are you sure you feel up to coming back so soon?" Guildea asked.

"I thank you for your concern, Doctor," Pettibone answered. "I had dinner with our lodge brother De Lancre on Tuesday. He said there is some disarray in the board proceedings at the orphanage."

"The old Academy of Perpetua. I forget what they are calling it now."

"Yes. The board did agree, however, to offer me the position of superintendent, and I have accepted the position."

"You are resigning?"

"Yes. Here is my official notice." Pettibone handed Guildea a neatly handwritten letter.

"I am surprised," Guildea said. "You now wish to run an orphanage. To care for children?"

"Yes. My experiences here have shown me that there lies my career. That is the thing in this world I am most *temperamentally* suited to do."

THE INTERCESSION OF
THE WHITE WORM

I
1898

THE 'WAR,' AS THE newspapers called it, was quickly over. More of a skirmish, actually, lasting only a few months. How could the fading empire of Spain have ever hoped to withstand the might of America, the world's newest great power? There was fear and anger in Manila at first, but many of Angelito's friends, mostly fellow teachers, were optimistic. But not all. "There is still ongoing resistance in the countryside," said Rafael, a history teacher. "The Americans are burning villages and torturing prisoners. Our students here come from wealthy families. They are not likely to resist unless they may profit from it."

"True, true," agreed Manuel and Ernesto.

"The people do not want to trade one colonizer for another," Rafael continued. Manuel and Ernesto agreed. Angelito shrugged.

"In time," he said, "I think that sentiment will change. There has never been a nation as rich in resources within its own boundaries and as potentially strong as America. Britain is dying a slow death. America is rising. I think the opportunities there could be staggering."

Rafael smiled at his friend. "I know you have been studying on this. Improving your English, too, I hear."

"Yes."

"And your American friend, the doctor..." Ernesto put in.

"Dr. Treves," Angelito said.

"Treves," Ernesto continued. "Has he convinced you to join him?"

"I think he has. He was grateful for the specimens I sent him. They helped him greatly in his experimental work. We have maintained a correspondence for two years now and he has asked me more than once to join him, as I have what he calls a special affinity and insight into his work."

"His work?" Manuel asked.

"Yes," Angelito refreshed his cup of salabat from the teapot on the table. "It's rather mysterious. It has to do with artificially engineered evolution and hereditary manipulation and...something to do with preventing organ rejection in transplant surgery." Angelito's friends looked perplexed. "As a teacher of natural sciences I was able to find him specimen sources for his research and my curiosity about all of it made a bond between us. I would be most gratified to work with him."

"What specimens did you send him?" Manuel asked as he stood. It was time for him to teach his geometry class.

"He wanted tissue samples from indigenous negritos, so I bartered for a tooth a young child had just lost and a lock of hair, and he also wanted eggs and larvae of *Teredo Navalis*," Angelito said.

"Ship worms?" Manuel frowned. "What in the world would he want with ship worms?"

II

It was obvious to Angelito that his young nephew was afraid. Although he was a teacher, Angelito had no particular love for children. But when the boy's parents were killed in a train accident in Batac, he felt honor-bound to take responsibility for him. Crisanto was seven years old now and traumatized by the loss of his family. He was fearful and nervous and seemingly dependent as a puppy upon his uncle, to protect him from the random cruelty of the world. "It is a frightening thing we are doing, Crisanto," Angelito said to the boy in an unusually patient tone, "but it is also a great adventure for us and an opportunity for me. Your life and mine will be so much better in the new land. You will make great friends you would never have known if we never left Manila."

"But how do we know we will like it there?"

"We will learn to, I promise you."

"But I won't know anyone..."

"We are going and you will accept it. I will not lose this opportunity because you do not want to go."

III

Colonel Pritchert of the US Army Eighth Corps had his headquarters on Aquino Street near Manila Bay. Angelito had helped Pritchert and his aides acquire herbs and roots to be used in homeopathic treatment of skin and stomach ailments among the American troops until medical supplies could arrive from Hawaii. A grateful Pritchert arranged passage for Angelito and Crisanto on the passenger steamer

Bihar bound for Brunei carrying three hundred pilgrims, then on to Honolulu.

The cabin Angelito shared with his nephew was very small and below the water line. There was fear in the boy's face as he sat on the edge of the lower berth. Crisanto began to gasp for air. "We don't have a window here. If the boat starts to sink we won't know it!" he said.

"Nothing will happen," Angelito said. "You need to accept what we are doing and enjoy it. I won't have you in a state of panic. To worry or not worry, the price is the same. We have three days to Brunei and another month to Honolulu. And I am guessing *another* month to San Francisco. I won't have you acting this way!"

On the first afternoon and most of the night, Crisanto was seasick. Angelito sat with him on his berth and, after the boy's stomach had settled, gave him laudanum to help him sleep. Late the next morning they made their way to the main deck. The three hundred pilgrim passengers were assembled there, immersed in their *Duhr,* the midday prayers. Observing the holy ritual, hundreds of souls kneeling, standing, raising hands aloft and murmuring prayers with eyes closed, distressed Crisanto. "What are they doing?" the boy asked.

"You have only spent time around Catholics in your life," Angelito said. "This adds to your education. They are praying. They are Mohammedans."

"Praying to Jesus?"

"No. They do not pray to Jesus."

"If they do not pray to Jesus, they will go to Hell, won't they? Do they want to go to Hell? Father Maldinado said this is a sin."

"The Father is wrong. Don't believe what priests tell you."

"I... want to go back to our cabin."

"Go, then. I am staying. I need the fresh air."

Crisanto stood still for a moment. He turned away from the worshippers. He silently moved behind his uncle and pressed against him. Angelito's first impulse was to push the boy away, but he didn't. He thought about the day the boy was born. Angelito's brother, Garibaldi, was a year younger and Crisanto was his first child. Angelito watched the expression on his brother's face as he looked down on his new son. It was an expression of a love that had no condition, was deep and complete. This surprised Angelito a little, he remembered. He had never felt such emotions, and assumed he never wanted to, yet a flicker of jealousy passed through him which he quickly pushed aside.

By the morning of the third day Crisanto had developed a small appetite. He ate a bit of the rice and fish his uncle brought him. That afternoon the *Bihar* made port at Muara and the pilgrims filed off the ship and onto the docks.

There were British ships in evidence everywhere in the port, and Angelito was able to quickly book passage to Honolulu on the transport of steam and sail, *Boudica.*

Boudica was larger than *Bihar,* and carried fewer passengers. Angelito and Crisanto secured a larger cabin than they had before, and one above the water line with a brass-rimmed porthole. Crisanto seemed mildly exhilarated to have a larger space and his seasickness abated until a squall was encountered on the fifth day out of port.

The storm grew in strength over the course of two hours. In the evening Angelito decided to make his way to the galley and bring back some food for a light meal. Fearing the violent pitching of the ship, Crisanto wanted to go with him. Angelito agreed, assuming the fearsome spectacle of the violent sea would dissuade the boy from any similar request in the future.

Stepping out of their cabin on the main deck of the starboard side, an enormous wave crashed against the hull of the ship, drenching Angelito and Crisanto. Angelito heard a slight cry from his nephew above the din of the tempest and in another second he saw that the boy was falling through the brass railing. Crisanto interlocked his fingers around the support, which stopped him from falling to the deck below, or possibly into the sea. For a moment, Angelito did not move. He watched the boy clinging to the railing, his small body thrashing with the pitching of the ship. It took the boy several terrified seconds to find his uncle on the wet deck. As they made eye contact and for a second after, Angelito moved to grasp Crisanto's small arm and pull him back onto the deck. The boy was crying hysterically. "I thought you had washed overboard," Angelito said emotionlessly. "I thought you were gone."

After two weeks at sea, conditions so becalmed that *Boudica* relied entirely on its engines to power it eastward. Two transports of the US Navy were spotted, on their way, Angelito assumed, to duty in the Philippines.

The voyage settled into a featureless monotony in the third week and Crisanto, finally recovered from the trauma of the storm, grew so accustomed to the routine that he occasionally ventured further away from the presumed protection and security of his uncle than he had before.

IV

Honolulu had the appearance of an occupied city. The streets were filled with Caucasian men and women in suits and western apparel mixing with robust brown people in native dress. And everywhere were American sailors and marines.

Colonel Pritchert had given Angelito a commendatory letter in Manila and after a two-day wait at the Rosas Hotel, Captain Maynard of the troop transport *USS Cayuga* found space for the two travelers on its return to San Francisco. Dr. Treves had written out detailed instructions for Angelito for the most efficient way to reach him in Ste. Odile. He was advised to take the Union Pacific Overland Route out of San Francisco across the mountains and plains to Council Bluffs on the Missouri River. There he would book passage on a steamboat down the river to the Mississippi, then book another to St. Louis and south to Ste. Odile.

Maynard told Angelito that with good weather the *Cayuga* should make San Francisco in good time. Studying a map of the United States in the cabin at night, Angelito was stunned that one country could be so large. He calculated it would take he and Crisanto another month of travelling to reach their destination.

V

Angelito could only afford to book them passage in the so-called emigrant cars at the rear of the trains. These were always densely packed and uncomfortable, with un-upholstered bench seats filled with poor newcomers from other lands looking for a better life in America. Most of these sat on the oaken benches with their coats draped over them, or rolled up to serve as a pillow. The discomfort, coupled with the coughing and snoring of the other passengers, plus the wailing of children, inconsolable in their weariness and sense of displacement, made the probability of rest unlikely for all but the soundest sleeper.

Crisanto slowly and selectively adapted to the food available to them. The meat-heavy diet disagreed with him at first but he gradually adjusted. Many of the other passengers appeared to be Chinese or Siamese and had to make the same acclimation. There were also Russians and Malay families and two Australians.

During a brief stop at North Platte Nebraska, Angelito bought a loaf of coarse bread and a sausage from a vendor on the platform. Back in the emigrant-car, he tore off a bit of the bread for his nephew. "Uncle," Crisanto said, "the man who checked our tickets called us Chinese."

"Chinese, Korean, Filipino, it's all the same to them," Angelito said. "They know little about our half of the world."

"We will be different from the people where we are going."

"Most of them, yes. But they have seen Asian people before. Chinese built these railroad tracks. Many Asians have made businesses or work in the houses of the rich Americans."

"Is Dr. Treves rich?"

"I think so. Well off, at least. Doctors are often well off. In any event, he was before he devoted himself to research."

"He doesn't take care of people anymore?"

"Not like Dr. Alba back in Manila. Dr. Treves wants to find ways to make people healthier, stronger, and in some ways, more than what they are."

"I don't understand."

"I don't either, not completely. But his curiosity fascinates me. I can learn much from him."

Crisanto was having difficulty chewing the coarse bread. "I had a dream, Uncle," he said. "I didn't want to tell you about it. I thought it might make you angry."

"Well?"

"In my dream you became best of friends with Dr. Treves. You liked him so much you stopped thinking about me. Dr. Treves didn't like me. He was mad that you brought me. In my dream he wanted to put me in a cage in a pond with just my head out of the water. Fish and other things could get into the cage and eat parts of me. There are sad people where we are going and monsters, I think. You wouldn't let him put me in the water, in the dream, but you almost did. One day you both were gone and you left me alone in a strange place."

Angelito's expression hardened. "I have told you many times: we are the same blood. I will *not* abandon you. I am not your father, though. I have no children for a reason. I wanted none. But I won't let you starve or leave you alone. You are like a tumor on my hip. You cannot cling to me as you do. I will not cast you off but you want more from me than I can give."

VI

Riverboat travel proved to be infinitely more comfortable than the trains. The boat they booked at Council Bluffs was the *Queen of Sheba*, and Angelito was able to secure them a small cabin on the boat's port side. Crisanto said he had never seen anything as beautiful as the riverboat with its white filigree and intricate scrollwork.

There was a dining room on the boat, but Angelito and Crisanto were not allowed to eat their meals there. Angelito was given no steward, and so he brought their food from the kitchen back to their cabin to eat. Crisanto was enjoying the cuisine now and did not look as skeletal as he had in San Francisco.

The boat was lodged briefly on a sandbar just northwest of a town called Rocheport. The passengers who were going on to St. Louis transferred to another boat, the *Lydia*, to continue their journey. In an hour they were off.

In a few days of relative comfort, they reached the great, bustling city, and Angelito and Crisanto boarded the sternwheeler *Seraphim* to finish their journey.

Angelito hoped that the boat would reach the landing at Ste. Odile before dark. But a long delay involving missing sacks of mail at a town called Kimmswick made that goal unlikely. The *Seraphim* arrived at Ste. Odile at a few minutes past eleven. Angelito watched on the Texas deck for the lights of the town, having been told by a mate that they would appear on the western bank.

Soon, in the darkness, Angelito saw the black hump of an island and the boat began to veer toward the right of it, by all appearances, heading toward an empty shore. The unfamiliar calls of whippoorwills drifted here and there above the dark barrier of forest on both banks of the wide river, mixed with the chirruping of tree frogs and other night sounds. There was a sliver of moon in the sky as the boat cleared the point of the island, and it illuminated a channel Angelito had not seen before. As the channel widened and the boat headed deeper into it, the few dim lamps of Ste. Odile became visible.

There were lanterns and oil lamps at the landing, and the boat sounded its whistle and made its way toward these slowly and carefully. Two men on the landing, stevedores, were the only people visible. The town looked abandoned and ancient, an empty, misplaced relic of an older time and an older country. The boat glided across the glass-like surface of the water and sidled against a rickety dock.

Angelito stepped back into their cabin and awakened Crisanto. They gathered their few things and went to the lower deck to disembark. They were the only passengers whose destination was Ste. Odile. As the stevedores unloaded two crates of hurricane lamps from the front deck of the boat, Angelito and Crisanto stepped from the gangplank onto the dock. Dr. Treves had given Angelito his address and directions from the landing to his house, but the town was so dark he felt disoriented and was unsure that he could read street signs. "Where do we go, Uncle?" Crisanto asked.

"I'm not sure," Angelito said. "Let's rest a while on this bench."

The boy collapsed onto the wooden bench and soon fell asleep. Angelito also sat on the often repainted bench, under a slight pool of lamplight. Soon the sleeping boy was leaning against his uncle. Angelito felt himself uncharacteristically paralyzed with doubt and uncertainty. He decided they would spend the night where they were and search for his mentor in the light of day.

VII

A packet whistle startled him awake. It was a foggy, damp morning on the river. Angelito could just make out the specter of the packet solidifying out of the mist to the north on the river. Stevedores were walking past the bench, heading toward the landing.

Angelito awakened the boy, who had hardly stirred all night. "We can find our way now," Angelito said. "Remember to only speak English."

The drive that led to the levee became a street called Mal Ardents. Angelito held the sluggish child's hand and they began walking west and up a cobblestoned hill. The air was damp and oppressive. Crisanto mumbled something about being hungry. Halfway up the slight hill, they encountered a street called Bosphorus, and turned south. There was little if any activity on the street. It was still far too early for shops and businesses to be opening. At the end of the first block, they found Rouen Street. "This is it," Angelito said. "His shingle should be halfway down."

The street was lined with once grand houses, each in different stages of repair and maintenance. They passed a fading mansion called Tranquille House and, two houses along, Angelito saw the shingle of Dr. Sirach Treves.

The house was a brooding sandstone pile sitting back some distance from the street. "These are like palaces," Crisanto marveled. "Are we going to live here?"

Angelito knocked timidly on the great oaken front door. After a minute or two, he knocked again and an elderly housekeeper opened the door, her face dark with disapproval and suspicion. "Are you from the laundry?" she asked. "I told you to never come this early."

"No, ma'am," Angelito said. "I am Angelito Belen from Manila. Dr. Treves is expecting us."

The old woman's gaze became even sharper. She opened the door and stepped aside. Angelito and Crisanto entered a dark vestibule. The old woman led the travelers into a nearby parlor containing a threadbare settee and two chairs near a fireplace. "Wait here," the old woman said.

Though sparsely furnished, the parlor had once been grand. Velvet draperies, sagging and tearing from their own weight, hung rotting alongside the single large window. Dusty animal skulls lined the marble mantelpiece. Angelito sat in one of the chairs, hearing the old fabric tear as he did. "He must be rich," Crisanto said.

"Be still!" Angelito admonished. "Stay out of the way and say nothing unless you are spoken to!"

In another moment, an older man with thinning hair and wearing a smoking jacket, entered the room. Angelito stood, and accepted Dr. Treves' embrace.

"Doctor," Angelito said. "Thank you for inviting us here."

"My friend Angelito," Treves said. "Finally we meet! So many services you have done for me. Now I can properly repay you. The eggs, the spores you sent me have proven most useful. Wait until you see how I have engineered them!"

"Engineered them? I am most anxious to see..."

"Well, this must be the boy you spoke of." Treves nodded toward Crisanto, who did not return his gaze.

"Crisanto, my nephew," Angelito said. "An orphan."

Treves shrugged and stepped out into the great entry area, indicating that his guests follow him. "Well, you said you were bringing him," he said. " And we will just have to make the best of it. Mrs. Dawson will show you to your room, or rooms if you wish private bedrooms..."

"Together," Crisanto said. Angelito flashed an angry glance at the child.

"Alright, together," Treves responded. "We will have breakfast there in the dining room in one hour. I trust you have eaten nothing yet this morning?"

VIII

The bedroom was a large one on the second floor with a bay window in the east wall. An enormous bed with a canopy dominated the room and Eastlake chairs and a settee sat in a corner. Crisanto was amazed at the dusty splendor of it all.

After a hurried breakfast of catfish, eggs, and fried potatoes, as Mrs. Dawson was clearing away the dishes, Treves all but took Angelito by the arm, anxious as he was to show his guest his laboratory. "May I come too?" Crisanto asked.

Treves shrugged. "I suppose so." Angelito opened his mouth to say something, but didn't.

At the rear of the great house, the three descended a dark stairway down to a brightly illuminated cellar. There were laboratory benches and tables, assorted glassware, cabinets and machinery. Treves opened a cabinet against a wall and removed a tray sectioned into water-filled compartments. He placed the tray on the central table. In each compartment were wriggling white larvae no more than an inch in length. "Here, my friend, is the most recent generation of the spores, the specimens of *Teredo Navalis* you sent me. They can hardly be called that anymore, though, because I have changed them."

"Changed them?" Angelito asked.

"These specimens are of a larger variety of *Teredo*, achieving a possible length of a meter or more. They have animalcules in their gut which allow them to digest wood fiber. I believe, however, that this fact is but a tangent off their true diet, tiny plankton and other microscopic marine creatures."

Angelito looked more closely at the larvae. Crisanto tried his best to see them over the high edge of the table. "How have you changed them?" Angelito asked.

"I am breeding them to change their diet," Treves smiled. "I am training them to eat...tumors!"

"Tumors?"

"Cancer. I have developed in them an appetite for these tumors. I have collected tumors removed in surgeries from a Dr. Landers and formerly from others, and I believe I now have a generation of worms that will seek out these masses in the human body and devour them."

"They will find the mass and eat it?" Angelito asked.

"Eat what?" Crisanto interrupted. In an instant, Angelito slapped the boy with the back of his hand.

"I told you to keep quiet!" Angelito snapped. Tears welled in Crisanto's eyes. His uncle had never struck him before.

"They will," Treves said, ignoring the interaction with a frown on his face. "They will eat the tumors. And I have a subject upon which to test the hypothesis. He is a vagrant. An old man with a cancer of the throat. Ralph Fernet is his name. He is nearing eighty and is more than willing to subject himself to this. Otherwise he has only a few months to live."

"Someone is going to die?" Crisanto mumbled to himself. As his uncle flashed his teeth in anger, the boy turned his back so he could not be slapped again.

"You go upstairs now. You've seen enough." Angelito's tone was sharp and impatient.

IX

Opening the door to the cellar, Crisanto nearly struck Mrs. Dawson who was still clearing away breakfast dishes. "You will need to stay out of my way, young man," the old woman said.

"I'm sorry, ma'am," the boy responded. "My uncle ordered me out of the cellar."

"Well, you should go to your room or...I suppose you can sit in any empty room downstairs, but you must stay out of my way."

"I will."

Mrs. Dawson stacked the dishes in the kitchen and returned to the hallway where Crisanto still stood. "I have a job for you," she said. "Would you like a task to occupy you?"

"Yes ma'am."

"You can wait on the porch for the grocery delivery. It should be here any time now. Bring the groceries inside. To the kitchen."

"Yes ma'am."

With some effort. Crisanto pulled open the heavy front door and stepped out onto the porch. He sat on the top marble step. The sun was partially visible above the rooftops to the east but the morning fog had still not burned off. It was odd to the boy that there was not a single person visible up or down the street. Back in Manila, the streets would be full of people at this hour. He did not notice the evidence of decay in many of the grand houses along Rouen Street, only their undoubted stature and elegance.

The clop-clopping of horse's hooves drifted out of the fog to the west. Soon the dark form of the animal emerged, pulling a black box of a delivery wagon behind it. The wagon was painted with white, yellow, and red ornamentation, and had the words LUPKE'S GROCERY emblazoned on the side. The wagon stopped two houses to the west at Tranquille House and a boy, who seemed to be wearing a hood over his head, got out and carried a small box to the front door. The boy quickly returned to the wagon. There was something pained and irregular about his gait.

In a few seconds the wagon stopped again at the curb in front of Crisanto. The driver was a very old man. As soon as he stopped the conveyance, his head drooped as if he had fallen immediately to sleep. The strange boy slid out of his seat and removed another box from the rear of the wagon. The box was larger than the first one and the boy seemed to be struggling with it. Crisanto stood and ran to the boy's aid. "Is it too heavy for you?" he said.

"I think so," the hooded boy said. "I have trouble with the big ones. I get punished if I drop one." His voice was indistinct, his words garbled and wet-sounding.

"I can help you." Crisanto grasped one end of the box, filled with eggs, coffee, bread, milk, a plucked chicken and many other things. The boys carried the box to the top of the steps and slid it onto the porch.

"Thank you," the hooded boy said. "I am supposed to carry it inside."

"I'll do it," Crisanto said. "You need to rest a little, I think." The hood the boy wore was made of canvas. The eye openings in it were large, but Crisanto saw no glint of eyes within them. "Why do you wear that on your head?"

"My face is gone," the boy said. "I live in the orphanage now and the Superintendent said I have childhood syphilis."

"What is that?"

"I got it from my mother. She ran off and my little brother died from it. I came to live with my uncle, but he won't have me. He put me in Phrygia House. They make children work and earn money if they can. They sent me to Lupke's. They said I have to wear this hood to hide myself. I can't see you very well, are you Chinese?"

"I'm Filipino. I am with my uncle now too. I don't know if he will keep me or not."

"What's Filipino?"

The driver of the wagon was fast asleep. The cart horse lowered his head and seemed to doze also. "Can you take off the hood?" Crisanto asked.

"No!" The boy was appalled by the question.

"What's your name?"

"Beau Garcon."

"That's an odd name. Let me see you. I think we could be friends, but I want to see you."

Beau Garcon sat in silence. "You won't want to be friends if you see me," he said. "No one is my friend at the orphanage. They make me wear this hood there now, too."

"It won't matter to me," Crisanto said.

Beau Garcon lifted his hood and dropped it onto his lap. Crisanto meant to hide his shock but he could not. The boy's nose and upper lip had fallen away, exposing serrated teeth, black gums, and a dark nasal hole. His skin was red and splotched with lesions. His eyes were hidden deep beneath swollen tissue surrounding them. "Oh," Crisanto said. "A disease did this to you?" Beau Garcon shook his head 'yes' and slipped his hood back on. "Well..." Crisanto continued. "It doesn't matter to me."

"Boy!" The elderly wagon driver had awakened. "What ere you a-lollygagging fer? We got deliveries!" Beau Garcon stood and ran, in his hobbled way, down to the wagon.

X

"This is Mr. Fernet," Treves said. "Mr. Ralph Fernet."

"How do you do, sir?" Angelito said to the old man.

Fernet nodded to his new acquaintance and leaned infirmly against the examination table. He was thin and pale, his skin splotched from months of exposure. His clothes were rags and hung on him. Angelito thought the old man could be a hundred years old. The odor emanating from him was almost intolerable. A swollen tumor bulged from his throat.

"First things first," Treves said. "In the rear corner is a bathtub with water drawn for you. You must bathe. Clean yourself. There is a gown hanging back there. Put it on afterwards. We will await you here."

Fernet disappeared into the rear lavatory. Treves removed the tray of larvae from the cabinet and placed them on the countertop. "We will try three of these to start," he said. "Put on your laboratory clothing and wash your hands well, my friend. Then we are ready for him."

Angelito did as he was told. Then he joined Treves in examining the contents of the tray. The larvae in their wet compartments were writhing actively.

"These are the larger *Teredo*," Treves said. "They have responded better to my breeding efforts."

"The ones that can reach a meter?"

"Yes. Once they have consumed the tumor, we will remove them."

In another half hour, Fernet returned to the laboratory, washed and wearing the surgical gown. "How do you feel, Ralph?" Treves asked.

"Well enough," Fernet responded. "Clean, I guess."

"On to the table, please. On your back." The old man slowly and painfully followed Treves' instruction. Once recumbent on the table, Treves lowered the top of the gown to reveal Fernet's swollen throat. "Just relax now," Treves continued. "All will be well. Angelito, if you please..."

Angelito retrieved a white cotton cloth and a corked bottle from the counter and placed these on the table in front of Treves. "This will put you to sleep, Ralph," Treves said as he saturated the cloth with the liquid and applied it to the old man's face. In a few seconds Fernet was unconscious.

"We will start with three applications," Treves said as he swabbed three areas around the base of Fernet's neck with alcohol. Then, with a fine scalpel, he sliced the three areas, making inch-long incisions. Finally he inserted a larva into each incision and stitched the openings with catgut. "They will grow quickly," Treves noted. "Fernet will live down here in an apartment I have prepared. We will watch his progress."

XI

The next delivery from Lupke's was on Friday. When the wagon stopped in front of Crisanto, and Beau Garcon removed a box of groceries from the back of it, the elderly driver suddenly drove off, leaving his helper on the curb. "What is he doing?" Crisanto asked.

"He forgets," Beau Garcon answered. "He probably thinks he's done for today. He forgets."

"You can wait with me until he comes back," Crisanto said, sitting on the top porch stair. Beau Garcon set his box down and sat next to him. "You can take your hood off if you want."

"I like to keep it on when I am outside."

"Well, it doesn't bother me if it's off."

"Okay." Beau-Garcon sat in silence for a moment. "It's hard for me to carry these boxes," he said, finally. "I'm not strong but the orphanage wants us to work."

"I wouldn't like that. I'm glad I have my uncle."

"I don't want to go back to Phrygia House. They are mean to me. They have no kindness. If I was stronger and didn't have to hide my face, I would run away."

Crisanto thought about his response for a moment. "You could stay here," he said.

"They wouldn't have me. My Uncle Louis told me nobody would have me."

"No one would know. This house is so big. There is an attic I have seen once. Mrs. Dawson never goes there and neither does Dr. Treves. We can get you up there when Dr. Treves and my uncle are working in the laboratory and Mrs. Dawson is napping. I will bring you food at night. I will try to take care of you."

"What would happen to you if you get caught?"

"I don't know. We don't have to think about that now."

Ralph Fernet was not recovering well. The incisions Treves had made to implant the larvae looked infected, though the creatures inside him were thriving. "His health has been ruined by years of malnutrition and alcohol," Treves said. "I should have foreseen this."

As Fernet lay on the examination table, skeletal and gaunt, the *Teredo* moved under his skin. The worms had tripled in length since they were implanted. They looked like swollen veins undulating under and through his epidermis.

One of the worms had circled past the anterior side of the tumor, and its head was now near Fernet's left ear. The old man moaned in pain as a second worm burrowed across his chest and the third progressed toward the jaw line. "Why aren't they attacking the tumor?" Angelito asked.

"They will find their way, given time. I am confident."

"Doctor, I don't think I can take this!" Fernet said. "God knows I appreciate what you are doing for me, but... the pain of it!"

"You have to be patient, Ralph," Treves said. "Your only alternative is to die. You must give us time." Treves and Angelito helped Fernet sit up on the table and onto his feet. The old man stumbled back toward his room. "He is proving to be a poor subject," Treves continued. "His body may be so deteriorated that the worms' sensory apparatus are confused. We will give him another week."

"We may need a younger subject? And a healthier one?" Angelito asked.

"Yes. If this experiment comes to nothing, Angelito, I won't be needing your assistance any further, I'm afraid."

Angelito was shocked by the statement. "But I thought I was to be your permanent assistant? For all your work."

"That was my original intention. I received notification this morning that a former patient of mine has filed a legal action against me. He agreed to an experimental medical treatment and it didn't turn out well."

"The Emlyn person you wrote about?"

"Yes. If I lose in court I will be ruined. I can revive my fortunes and reputation in St. Louis if this work we are doing succeeds...I expect. I alone have bred these creatures. I have the secret to this new technique. It's all just happened. I'm sorry, but there it is."

Angelito was speechless for a moment. "I can't go back to Manila. There is nothing for me there anymore. And the boy..."

"You should not have brought him." Treves' voice was stern. "I don't know why you did. This is no home for a child. You should consider placing him in the orphanage. That will put him out of your thoughts so that you may direct *all* your attention toward work that will secure our futures."

"Yes," Angelito said.

XII

Crisanto found that the only adult in the house who seemed to notice his coming and going, was Mrs. Dawson. He discovered it was easier to carry food to his friend in the attic than he expected. The old woman had a diminished capacity to clean house and prepare meals. She napped intermittently and rarely climbed the stairs except to tidy the bedrooms on the second floor, a task she undertook no more than twice a month.

Beau Garcon seemed terrified at his own good fortune. "This place is all my own," he marveled. "All of this space. I am safe and hidden." He ate the bread and cheese Crisanto had brought him.

"It's so hot up here," Crisanto said. "I'll push open the windows." After much effort, he managed to slightly open the two east-facing dormers and their opposites on the west wall. Beau Garcon had become his responsibility, and he found himself thinking often about his charge and his needs. Crisanto rarely saw his Uncle Angelito, working as he did, long hours in the laboratory, but he found that he felt the loss of this, the security and sense of protection, less and less as time went on. "I'll bring a bucket of fresh water for you when I can and you can have some of my clothes. You are older than me but I think my clothes will fit. The orphanage must be wondering what happened to you."

"No. Children disappear from there, or die. No one mentions it. How long can I stay here?"

"I heard of a mission across the river. A hospital for children. The town is called Prairie du Rocher. It's run by Jesuits and nuns. It's for children with the worst sicknesses. St. Philomena, it's called. Mrs. Dawson was talking to our neighbor about it. That lady's grandson is a Mongolian idiot, but they take good care of him and he is happy there, she said. If we could get across the river..."

XIII

Ralph Fremet no longer had the ability to speak. The tumor on his throat had grown, as had the specimens inside him. One of the worms had discovered the thyroid mass and by all appearances was feeding upon it. Another worm had moved beyond the right jawline and coiled its more than twelve-inch length across the man's face and cranium. The third creature formed a gelatinous serpentine ridge which was slowly undulating across the chest and abdomen. Fremet drifted into a comatose state.

As Treves and Angelito watched, the specimen on Fremet;s face burrowed into the crater of the man's eye socket. The eyeball began to bulge as the worm pressed against it inside. In a second a slight sucking accompanied the eyeball as it burst from the socket, spattering blood and black fluid. Attached to its stringy muscles, the eyeball lolled across Fremet's face as the horned white head of the worm emerged from the socket. Fremet whimpered and gasped for air.

Treves and Angelito re-positioned the tiny man on the examination table. "We will remove this worm and the abdominal *Teredo*," Treves said. "This was a mistake, using this old man. We have a new generation of larvae even more specialized to our needs and fresh cancer cells coming from the hospital later today. And these will be the last. My supplier, Dr. Landers, retires tomorrow."

Ralph Fremet coughed, spattering blood on his face and on the tabletop, and died. Angelito felt for a pulse. "A shame we couldn't help him," he said. "I suppose we will have to notify the sheriff or coroner. We must report this."

"No," Treves said. "He was a destitute man with no home or connections. It will be simpler to just dispose of him. Much simpler. No one will miss him, and no one will question our work here."

Angelito was shocked at the suggestion. "But this man has died."

"What are you doing down here?" Treves barked. Angelito turned and saw Crisanto standing at the foot of the staircase. "You were told to never come down here!" Treves went on.

The boy looked cornered and afraid. "I wanted another blanket," he said. "Mrs. Dawson is asleep. I couldn't wake her."

Angelito's anger burst from him suddenly. "You shouldn't be here. I should have never brought you! Go upstairs!" The boy ran up the staircase.

"Well, there it is," Treves said.

"He will say nothing," Angelito said. "He knows no one. He may have heard nothing."

"What child can keep his mouth shut? This is brilliant, Angelito, just brilliant!"

"He is dependent on me and fears abandonment. I will tell him if he says a word I will be taken away and he will be alone."

"I can't have ignorant city officials blocking my work. You will need to make a decision, my friend." Treves walked to a nearby desk chair and collapsed into it. "As it turns out, you have jeopardized my researches and my very freedom by bringing this boy with you. You can repent that error if you wish to stay with me here and stay in this country."

Angelito was apprehensive. "What do you mean, Doctor?"

"We need a new subject no later than tomorrow morning if the cancer cells I am receiving are to be of use. We will use the boy. He is young and healthy. It will be painful but he will come through it, most likely."

"He could die."

"But we will gain data in the process. You have no love for him. No one knows he is here. I may not be able to acquire tumors in future. I need this subject by tomorrow."

XIV

Crisanto was not in their bedroom. Angelito looked into Mrs. Dawson's room and found her asleep, as his nephew had said. As he returned to the staircase to descend and look outside, he heard the creak of a board in the floor above him. "Crisanto!" he called up the dark staircase. No response. Angelito ran up the stairs to the third-floor hallway. He found the attic door ajar. He pushed the door open and heard a faint gasp waft down from above him.

In the gloom of the attic, under a dormer in the far wall, Angelito saw his nephew crouching on the floor. "What is this?" Angelito demanded. Crisanto sprang to his feet and ran to his uncle, embracing him around his waist. "What are you doing up here?" Angelito was startled by his nephew's sudden and somehow affected embrace.

"I am out of the way here," Crisanto said. "I must stay out of sight of Mrs. Dawson and you and Dr. Treves. I am doing nothing wrong. I know if I do you will send back me to Manila...alone."

Angelito scowled down at his nephew. "You depend too much on me. I am not made for it. Yes, I could send you home if I chose. That is up to you."

"Up to me?"

"You can help Dr. Treves and me. First by never repeating that a man died downstairs."

"I would say nothing."

"And also." Angelito had to muster the resolve to say it. "You can help with the experiment. The research."

"How?"

"Dr. Treves thinks you would make a good subject for the larvae."

"But...don't they grow? Wouldn't they hurt me?"

"All that is true." Angelito's tone turned to one of anger. "It could hurt. You might not even...you would at least be of some use for once! I can force you if I want. I *could*. But you are my brother's child, I..."

A gasp of air drifted out from a corner shadow. Crisanto looked toward the sound in terror.

"Who is there?" Angelito demanded. A ragged form stepped out of the gloom: a boy with a hood covering his head. "Who are you?"

A garbled murmur came from under the hood. "It is Beau Garcon," Crisanto said. "My friend. He has a disease. He needs help. I have been helping him."

Angelito pulled the hood from Beau Garcon's head. Angelito gasped and stepped back in horror. "By all the saints!" he said. Tears nearly welled in his eyes. He tried to suppress them. "He is a leper!" he exclaimed.

"No," Crisanto said. "It is called childhood sipulus. He says he can't give it to anyone else."

"*You* have been caring for him?"

"Yes. He ran away from the orphanage."

"Then he must return there," Angelito insisted. "Treves won't stand for this."

"No," Crisanto's tone was surprisingly firm. "I take care of him now. They are cruel at the orphanage. They treat him as a burden."

"He takes care of me," Beau Garcon mumbled.

"There is a hospital across the river," Crisanto continued. "St. Philomena. They care for children. I am taking him there. No one but me will help him."

"I am not going to some charity hospital with you..." Angelito said.

"I didn't ask you, Uncle," Crisanto replied. "I will do it myself. He can live there and I will look after him. I want to remind them to be kind to him."

Angelito looked down at his nephew for a moment. The boy returned the gaze devoid of doubt or expectation. Crisanto then looked at Beau Garcon with the same affection, Angelito thought, that his dead brother had once shown to his infant son. To Angelito, his nephew seemed years older than he had a moment before. He felt an instantaneous disconnection from the child, a separation and distance that overwhelmed him with a desolate sense of emptiness and abandonment.

Angelito reached into his trousers pocket. He withdrew his leather money belt. From it he removed several folded dollar bills and five silver dollars. He gave the money to Crisanto. "The ferry," he said. "You need money for the ferryman."

XV

The next morning Angelito found Dr. Treves in the laboratory tending to his larvae. "I expected you a half hour ago," Treves said.

"I am sorry to be late," Angelito responded. "I wanted to bathe this morning."

"As you wish. The tumor samples arrived last night as promised. These are the last ones I can obtain from the hospital. Dr. Landers retires today. Where is our subject?"

Angelito removed his shirt and positioned himself on the examination table. "Just here, Doctor. You will find the chloroform in that cabinet."

BURNED MAN
AT NIGHT

AMBRUS WAS GRATEFUL THAT the Americans had spared his life. Grateful, at least, in those moments when his anger and outrage faded temporarily away. He was one of several elderly Hungarian widows and widowers who were not brutalized and run out of town in the riot of 1917 when the conscription of Americans for the army started. He was too decrepit to take any young man's job who was away at war. He was harmless, alone, and he distilled the pálinka brandy the townspeople had developed a taste for.

Ambrus' daughter and son-in-law were not so lucky. When the lead-miners in town got word of the conscription and learned that the Hungarian immigrants Osage Lead had brought in for cheap labor were not subject to the draft for the war in Europe, they began a rampage through the immigrant neighborhoods. Ambrus' daughter Mariska and her husband died trying to save their home from the fire the rioters had started. Their infant daughter, Hajnal, was saved by neighbors. It was up to Ambrus to raise her.

Hajnal was twelve now. She loved to hear her grandfather's stories about her dead parents. She loved their wedding photograph and thought her mother beautiful. "If I can be as beautiful as my mother someday, I will be happy," she said.

"You will be that beautiful and that virtuous and strong...I know you will," Ambrus answered.

"That is what I will pray for," the girl said.

Ambrus decided he would introduce his granddaughter to the ways of *Jòindulatú Boszarkány*, the craft of the Benevolent Witch. Ambrus' late sister-in-law knew these crafts and his brother, Csepel, who had vanished two summers ago, had been her *Gyám*, or guardian. Ambrus resolved, because of her young age, to teach Hajnal only such few secrets as he knew were beneficial and save those dark arts, which inevitably accompany such insights, for later years. Much too soon to reveal to the girl the world of vengeful spirits, demons, and *Ordög*, the Dark Master. There were still a few Hungarians left in town after the purge and they had no *Boszarkány*. Once trained,

Hajnal would keep that connection to the past for them. And Ambrus, for as long as he was able, would be her *Gyám.*

Hajnal's curiosity about nature and secret things seemed limitless. Ambrus had always kept an herbal garden and a garden of forbidden plants, in case they were ever needed. He cultivated henbane, poppy, mandragora, and other nightshades, asafetida, and many other more congenial herbs.

The hills across the road to the east of Ambrus' property, as well as the flat lands to the west, were heavily wooded and full of game. On Saturday afternoons and Sundays, which were the lead-miners' free time, the popping of rifles and the boom of shotguns could be heard. Esau Farren's property was a quarter mile north of Ambrus', along the LaMotte Road. Esau was a widower with a curved spine who could do no work more demanding than tending his small garden. Esau's sons Rayford, age eighteen, and Loomis, age twenty, as well as their cousin Nebo, age nineteen, lived with him and worked in the lead mines at Lesterton.

The boys hunted squirrels and raccoons near Ambrus' property. They always greeted Ambrus and Hajnal warmly if they saw them when they emerged from the tree line with their evening's kill. "How you-uns a-doin' tonight?" Loomis said. It was Holy Saturday and Ambrus and Hajnal were resting on the porch.

"Very well, Mr. Farren," Ambrus responded. "Thank you for asking."

"And what about you, girly?" Loomis said to Hajnal. She always seemed discomfited to be spoken to.

"I am fine. Fine, thank you."

"Hope the shootin' don't bother you-uns," Rayford chimed in. One of the three of the boys had asked this question dozens of times.

"No, my granddaughter and I thank you for your concern."

For dinner on Easter Sunday, Ambrus made chicken paprikash, which was Hajnal's favorite. After the meal, the child helped with washing the dishes and replacing them in the cupboards. "Those Farrens always seem like they are making fun of us," Hajnal said.

"It does seem so, doesn't it?" Ambrus responded. "So long as they keep their distance."

The sun was fully set as Ambrus cleaned the last skillet. He glanced out the window above the sink toward the western woods. In the distance, meandering among the dark expanse of tree trunks, Ambrus saw an odd light flickering. The light seemed to grow and shrink from a tiny spot to something much larger as it vanished and reappeared between the trunks. The color of the light changed from blue to white to orange and then to the color of raw meat, for twenty or thirty seconds until it disappeared entirely.

"What is it, grandfather?" Hajnal asked.

"Nothing. A light of some kind out in the woods. Will-o-the-Wisp." He smiled down at her. "Made me think of my brother for some reason."

"The one who vanished?"

"Yes. Shall we read a little before bedtime?"

Ambrus didn't send Hajnal to school. The county and the town didn't keep track of children from Hungarian families. Ambrus had taught his granddaughter the alphabet and numbers and he read to her and with her every day. The Sunday after Easter, Ambrus twisted his ankle stepping off his back porch to collect eggs from the henhouse. The ankle started to swell and Hajnal heated a pail of water with salts for him to soak it in. After an hour, the ankle was still very tender and Ambrus knew he could not put weight on it. "Hajnal," he said as he elevated his foot onto a stool. "You know where old Elek lives?"

"Yes. In the boarding house by the train tracks. Mrs' Hobbs' house. Remember? I have been there a lot."

"Yes. He paid me for a bottle of pálinka. Will you take it to him this morning?"

Hajnal's eyes brightened and she shook her head 'yes'. Ambrus knew she loved to walk to the boarding house and talk with Mrs. Hobbs, who always gave her hard candy. "One of those bottles by the breadbox," Ambrus said. "Take one of those and tell him I am sorry for the delay. You hurry home afterward. We are doing arithmetic today."

"I will!" Hajnal smiled as she took one of the bottles of brandy and put it in her small haversack hanging near the door. "I won't be too long," she said as she scurried out the front door.

Ambrus lowered his foot back into the salt water and left it there until the water became tepid. His ankle looked a little swollen, but he found he could put weight on it. He limped to the front of the house to a window and looked up the road toward the north. Hajnal still had not returned. He thought she must be enjoying her talk with Mrs. Hobbs.

Ambrus poured himself a small glass of brandy from an opened bottle. He made his way out to the front porch and sat in his rocker to watch the road. When he sipped his brandy on the porch he often thought of Lillafüred, his home back in Hungary. His late brother and sister-in-law were from there, as were most of his countrymen who were settled in this area. Most were placed in housing built and owned by the lead company.

The Hungarians kept many of their traditions alive, though it was quickly clear that the Americans did not approve of their Old World ways: the traces of the old religion they still observed, and their superstitions. There had even been rumors of a vampire a few years before, when some few local children became anemic and several died. The conscription riot was the culmination of all the resentment.

Hajnal would ask her grandfather about the old world in the evenings as they sat on the porch. "The heat here is terrible," the old man had told the child the night before. "There is nothing like this back home, back in the mountains. Oppressive heat and bitter winters here."

"And the people here don't like the festivals we have and the old religion," Hajnal said.

"No."

"Grandfather, have you ever seen the Burned Man?"

"You heard about the Burned Man?"

"Yes. Old Elek told me. The last time I took brandy to him. You said you saw light in the woods before. You called it Will-o-the-Wisp. I wondered if that's the same as the Burned Man?"

"People have their secrets," Ambrus said after a long pause. "Rumors start and it is often hard to know what is true and what isn't. My brother Csepel was attuned to such things. He and his wife. Christian Cabala, old knowledge borrowed from the Hebrews. I don't know how much is true."

"He burned up, didn't he? Uncle Csespel?"

"Yes. Fell into a fire or was thrown...and ran off ablaze. Never seen again."

Ambrus sipped his brandy. "Elek should not talk about such things to you." Ambrus realized he said this out loud. To no one. Hajnal had still not returned. The old man stood. Panic was seizing him. Hajnal would never stay away this long. Ambrus hobbled to his tomato patch beside his house. He pulled one of the stakes out of the ground to use as a walking stick.

After a few minutes' walking north on the dusty road, Ambrus' injured ankle was throbbing. As he approached his neighbor's property, he saw a child's footprint in the dust beside the road. There were no more footprints beyond it. He looked toward Esau Farren's farmhouse. All was dark and their truck was missing. In the grass near the footprint, Ambrus found a cork. It was of the type he used in his brandy bottles. Ambrus decided to walk up the drive and knock on the Farrens' door. There was no answer. The old man made his way back to the road and called his grandaughter's name into the woods and across the fields a few times. The sun was going down. He continued north along the road, calling into the darkening forest every few seconds.

By the time Ambrus reached the boarding house he was exhausted and drenched with sweat. He climbed the rotting steps to the front door. It was locked. Mrs. Hobbs had already gone to bed. Ambrus pounded on the door. After a few minutes, Mrs. Hobbs, in her bathrobe, answered the door. "My goodness, Mr. Horvath! What is it?" She was a thin woman in her late 40's who looked much older than her years.

"I am sorry to disturb you, Mrs. Hobbs. Have you seen my granddaughter today? Have you seen Hajnal?"

"No...she ain't been here. She is missing?"

"I sent her here this morning. With pálinka for Elek."

"Oh, Lord!" Concern darkened Mrs. Hobbs' face. "Come in, come in. We'll call the sheriff."

Within an hour Sheriff Allard and two deputies from Ste. Odile arrived at the boarding house. Allard decided to retrace the walk from the boarding house back to Ambrus' home. Ambrus accompanied them, though the old man was exhausted and his ankle had greatly swollen. The deputies concentrated on the wooded areas east of the road. Allard and Ambrus scoured the west side.

One of the deputies, the younger of the two, had roamed some one hundred feet off the road. He had become invisible in the darkness except for his flashlight. "Sheriff!" the young man called. "I got a bottle over here."

Allard helped Ambrus make his way through the undergrowth toward the young deputy. The young man shown his flashlight on the ground. The light glinted off a clear glass bottle. Allard picked it up. "That's one of my bottles...yes!" Ambrus said. "I found the cork on the roadside just opposite here."

Allard scoured the ground, strewn with dry leaves and oak branches. A small brown object protruded from the ground cover near a log. Ambrus' heart sank when he recognized it to be a woven leather *bochkor* or child's sandal. Emerging from this and disappearing into the leaves was a pallid and swollen child's foot and ankle.

The coroner's report came the next evening. Allard drove out to Ambrus' home as soon as he received it. Hajnal had been attacked by two or more assailants. She had been sexually assaulted, beaten and strangled. The old man found himself swooning as Allard read the words. Ambrus began to cry hysterically. He lost his balance and fell to the floor. *"Nem tudom elképzelni hogy ezt elviselte volna!* I cannot imagine her enduring that!" he wailed. "I can't think of my girl...the terror she felt. She had no understanding of such...brutalized! The terror she felt!"

Allard sat with the old man for another hour. Ambrus' anguish advanced and diminished all that time. His grief would reach a peak, then trail off gradually, only to revive itself as the horror of the imagined scene reconstituted in his mind. "I'm gonna send one of the boys out tomorrow and maybe the next day to check on you," Allard said as he walked to the door. "You'll get through this. We'll find the sons o' bitches."

"Sheriff Allard," Ambrus said, composing himself for a moment. "Surely you know, as I know, who *must* have done this?"

Allard nodded. "I have my suspicions. I am going to talk to the Farrens right now. You stay away from them. Don't talk to them. Don't accuse them. Try to get some rest."

Ambrus sat in his front room all night. The burr of tree frogs and insects and the calls of the whippoorwills faded away as dawn approached. He didn't know how he would face the day to come: the terrible silence, the torture of his thoughts, and the horrendous emptiness of the world. He could not eat. He sipped water occasionally.

He felt exhausted and depleted but could not rest. His stomach pained him from hunger which transitioned to nausea and back again, a cycle he didn't feel he could tolerate for long. Late in the morning the younger of Allard's deputies stopped in to check on Ambrus. "The Farrens are coming in for questioning today," he said. "They got an alibi from some fellow in Lesterton, but nobody else can verify."

"My girl is at Boyer's now?"

"Yes. They are preparing her. Will be a closed casket. Funeral at Church of the Holy Mandillion Thursday. Nine AM. Her place is being prepared in the church cemetery." The young deputy moved toward the door. He paused. "Have you got a gun, Mr. Horvath?"

"Yes. A shotgun."

"Keep it handy for a while yet. Don't look for trouble but be ready just in case."

In the evening Ambrus fried himself an egg, which he ate with a little dry bread. Though he felt completely enfeebled, he knew he could not sleep. He moved out to the porch and sat in his chair to feel the breeze and listen to the night sounds.

After an hour, the burr of the tree frogs suddenly stopped. Out in the dark forest across the road, Ambrus heard branches snap as though under footsteps. He had left his shotgun inside. He stood, but before he could return to the house, he saw a flicker of light out amongst the tree trunks. He stood still. The light moved slowly toward the north, then stopped. It floated toward the southwest, then seemed to be coming directly toward him. He could not look away from the light. The light turned orange and then red, then the color of burned flesh. Ambrus felt as though his eyes suddenly opened. "Csepel," he said, "Csepel, my brother. It's you?"

Ambrus felt nearly overcome with emotion. He realized that his revelation about the light in the forest could not come until he was shattered enough to receive it. With the death of his precious Hajnal, he had been made ready. He hobbled across the road and into the woods opposite his property. The dark tangle of undergrowth slowed his progress and his injured foot ached. He stopped to rest against a tree trunk. He could not see the light and for a moment became confused about in which direction it lay.

As he rested against the tree trunk, a breeze stirred. It was an unusually warm draft. Its warmth surprised him.

"Ambrus..." The name was whispered on the advancing current. "Brother."

The bushes rustled a little to his left. Then the glow slowly revived, and the light moved through the old-growth hardwoods some twenty feet from him. He *could* have imagined the whispered words, real as they seemed when he heard them. He rejected this thought. He was then terrified to accept that there was a sentient being nearby, dark one moment and aflame the next, maneuvering, entwining effortlessly through the undergrowth. If he were wrong and the entity was not his brother, then it could only be the demon Ordög, there to torment him in his grief.

"*Hello?*" Ambrus whispered. "Hello," more loudly.

"Your pain..." the zephyr gasped.

"What?"

"Your pain brings me close. Because I am the Guardian."

"A Guardian! Csespel! It *is* you!"

"I am. I am...brother."

"Yes. Zsofia your wife was *boszarkany*. And you protected her. You were *gyam*."

"The Guardian. You have forgotten the old way, but you are still one with it."

"Yes, I am. Now more than ever. An abomination has happened. Unspeakable. Unimaginable. There can be no recompense to equal that abomination." The form of the Burned Man was more substantial now. The seared and blistered flesh seemed wrapped in flame and oozing the bubbling life fluids erupting from the immolation.

"What will give peace to you...and to the desecrated child?"

Esau Farren seemed smaller, more oppressed by his pain than when Ambrus had last seen him. His shoulders were hunched, his spine twisted, his face dark and suspicious when he opened the door. "Ambrus," the old man said. "Nebo said you was a-comin'."

"Yes. He is kindly letting me borrow his dog, and will teach her to hunt with me."

"Guess you better come in. I can't stand around for long. My back is too bad." Esau turned and hobbled back to a rocking chair near their Franklin stove. He sat painfully. "What you got there?"

"Brandy," Ambrus said. He sat the bottle on the kitchen table. "Where is Nebo?"

"Feedin' the hogs, I guess. He'll be back soon."

"Where are the other boys?" Ambrus looked out at the road through the house's only window.

"Stayed in town tonight. Don't know if they're comin' home or not. Sometime of a weekend they just stay in town until work on Monday. I'd take a hit of that likker if you was of a mind to find me a cup."

"Of course." Ambrus took a coffee cup from a shelf over the kitchen table. He opened the brandy and poured. He carried the cup to the crippled man.

"This'll do the trick!" Esau gulped the brandy. "I...uh. Sorry to hear about your little girl. Just terrible. The things people do! Hope they catch the sons o' bitches."

"They won't," Ambrus scowled. "Out in the country like this. Yes, it was more than one attacker. Country sheriff... I don't think they will try very hard to make things right."

"Well, you never know. So you wanna start huntin' coons at night at your age, do you?"

"Yes. My nights are more restless now. I thought I might use my time better, other than staring at the wall and thinking too much. And I could have more meat. I can't afford meat very often. I hear raccoon is good."

"Greasy and gamey, if you ast me. You get used to it, though." Esau shifted in his chair and winced in pain. "Well, don't keep my boy out too late. I'm just all but helpless here. Won't be long I won't be able to do for myself at all."

"I won't."

The back door opened and Nebo stepped in. He was the tallest of the three boys. His overalls were covered in mud and hay particles. A rank odor emanating from him quickly filled the room. He seemed surprised to see Ambrus. "Oh," he said. "I didn't know if you'd really show up."

"Yes," answered Ambrus. "You are showing me how to hunt raccoons. I can give you ten dollars for every lesson. If it goes well tonight, I'll give you another ten in advance."

"Iff'n you got twenty dollar to throw away," Esau put in, "I'd be damned iff'n I would't buy me a big old ham and some baloney instead of payin' this layabout to teach you to hunt, whether he my nephew or no..."

Nebo's face brightened. "Ain't much lesson to it. But, I can sure use the money. I'll get old Esme. She's my best coon dog. I seen her climb up a tree and snatch one of the little bohunkus' off'n a limb!"

"That's fine. That's good," Ambrus said. "You know the clearing, the glade where those old stone steps are?"

"That old cabin? Amsel. The Amsel place."

"Yes. I will meet you there. I have changed my mind about shooting tonight. I want to fetch my shotgun. I'll meet you there. At the steps."

It was nearly two hours before Ambrus appeared at the clearing. He carried his lantern. As he expected, Nebo was still waiting for him. "I about give up on ye," Nebo said. Esme, the old coonhound, skittered away from Ambrus, her head bobbing up and down in what seemed like fear and confusion. She yipped and barked and hid herself behind the ash tree against which Nebo was leaning. "Esme, shaddup!" Nebo yelled. "Shaddup now!"

The dog whimpered and bolted away toward the road and home.

"God dammit, Esme! Git back here! Son of a bitch, what's wrong with her?" He looked over at Ambrus. "Crazy ol' dog. She ain't afraid of nothin'. Don't know why you skeered her. Say... you didn't even bring your gun. You was gonna fetch your gun."

"I didn't bring it."

"Well what you been doin' for almost two hour? If we gonna hunt together and you say you're gonna do a thing, I expect you to do it!"

Ambrus smiled at him. An ossified, mirthless smile, lighted invidiously by the lantern now on the ground below him. Terror washed over Nebo's face. "*Egett ember. Itt az ideje,*" Ambrus said.

"What? What the Hell did you say?"

The old man only smiled more in response, and closed his eyes. "*Itta az ideje,*" he repeated.

A yellow glow flickered behind the ash tree. A moan oozed through the branches. In a burnt form of orange flesh congealing in the humid air, an eye drifted past, partially obscured by a vane of burned tissue at its inner corner. Two white teeth glistened below this for a second as the manifesting form wrapped itself around the paralyzed Nebo.

Nebo screamed.

The burning form dragged the boy up the tree trunk. Nebo resisted for no more than a second. His overalls were now afire. He gurgled as wet air was forced out of his lungs. The Guardian lifted the boy to a large branch and wedged his neck in its fork. The flesh could be heard blistering and popping. There the hulking form hung until burning fragments of clothing began to fall away, and the smoldering body snapped loose from its head and fell to the ground. Ambrus watched in placid satisfaction. He had been excited and jubilant at first, but now he was calm. Justice had been served. He turned and faced the west. He must return to the Farrens' farmhouse. He had blockaded the window and two doors of the house so the old man could not escape. He should be dead by now. He had faced the Guardian alone and in terror, but must surely be dead by now.

The other boys, whenever they returned home, would only see a wisp of smoke arising over the roof. When they saw the barriers and blockades Ambrus had made, they would panic. Ambrus needed to be there when they arrived.

About
JOHN S. McFARLAND

JOHN S. McFARLAND'S short stories have appeared in numerous journals, in both mainstream and horror genres. His tales have been collected with stories by Stephen King, H. P. Lovecraft, Robert Bloch and Richard Matheson. His work has been praised by *Publishers Weekly*, *Kirkus*, and such writers as Ramsey Campbell, T. E. D. Klein, Dacre Stoker, and Philip Fracassi. He has been called "A great, undiscovered voice in horror fiction," his work lauded as "Gifts sprung from a dark chest full of wonders." McFarland's horror novel

The Black Garden was published in 2010 to universal praise, and his young reader series about Bigfoot, *Annette: A Big, Hairy Mom,* is in print in three languages. His story collection *The Dark Walk Forward,* appeared in a German-language edition in 2024, and a chapbook he will share with Ramsey Campbell will appear next year. *Burned Man at Night* is his third story collection.

www.ingramcontent.com/pod-product-compliance
Lightning Source LLC
Chambersburg PA
CBHW020645250626
47154CB00008B/2821